P9-CRX-261

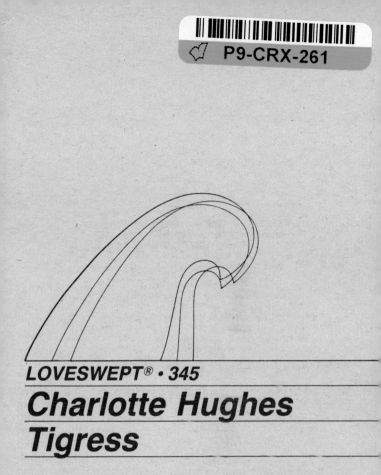

LOVESWEPT® • 345

Charlotte Hughes
Tigress

BANTAM BOOKS
NEW YORK • TORONTO • LONDON • SYDNEY • AUCKLAND

TIGRESS
A Bantam Book / August 1989

*LOVESWEPT® and the wave device are registered
trademarks of Bantam Books, a division of
Bantam Doubleday Dell Publishing Group, Inc.
Registered in U.S. Patent
and Trademark Office and elsewhere.*

All rights reserved.
Copyright © 1989 by Charlotte Hughes.
Cover art copyright © 1989 by Hal Frenck.
*No part of this book may be reproduced or transmitted
in any form or by any means, electronic or mechanical,
including photocopying, recording, or by any information
storage and retrieval system, without permission in
writing from the publisher.*
For information address: Bantam Books.

*If you would be interested in receiving protective vinyl
covers for your Loveswept books, please write to this address
for information:*

*Loveswept
Bantam Books
P.O. Box 985
Hicksville, NY 11802*

ISBN 0-553-22018-7

Published simultaneously in the United States and Canada

---

*Bantam Books are published by Bantam Books, a division
of Bantam Doubleday Dell Publishing Group, Inc. Its trademark, consisting of the words "Bantam Books" and the
portrayal of a rooster, is Registered in U.S. Patent and
Trademark Office and in other countries. Marca Registrada.
Bantam Books, 666 Fifth Avenue, New York, New York 10103.*

PRINTED IN THE UNITED STATES OF AMERICA

O   0 9 8 7 6 5 4 3 2 1

Suddenly the water in the shower turned icy cold, and Natalie shrieked. Nick came running. . . .

"What are you doing in there?" he yelled. She was hidden from him by the frosted glass doors, but he couldn't get the image of her lovely body out of his mind.

"The door's stuck, and the water got cold, and I can't get out. Please hand me my towel," she said in a strained voice, trying to keep her dignity.

He passed the towel overhead, and struggled for several minutes to get the door back on its track. When he slid it open, he stifled the urge to laugh. Natalie looked like a wet mouse standing there dripping.

"Lady, do you always have this much trouble, or have I caught you at a bad time?" She didn't answer, and for a moment all he could do was stare. The soapy sheen on her body made his mouth go dry.

"Could you please . . . help me out?" she asked, terrified of slipping. She held out her hand. But Nick ignored it and scooped her easily from the tub.

"This wasn't what I had in mind," she said, sounding annoyed, but unable to pull away.

Nick smiled. "I was trying to prevent you from falling," he said, still holding her in his arms. She sank against him, seeking his heat. He felt her tremble, and as crazy as it sounded, he wanted to protect her, comfort her . . . and more. As he lowered his lips to hers, he faced the truth. He had only to touch her to lose himself, and secretly he'd known that all along. . . .

WHAT ARE *LOVESWEPT* ROMANCES?

They are stories of true romance and touching emotion. We believe those two very important ingredients are constants in our highly sensual and very believable stories in the *LOVESWEPT* line. Our goal is to give you, the reader, stories of consistently high quality that may sometimes make you laugh, sometimes make you cry, but are always fresh and creative and contain many delightful surprises within their pages.

Most romance fans read an enormous number of books. Those they truly love, they keep. Others may be traded with friends and soon forgotten. We hope that each *LOVESWEPT* romance will be a treasure—a "keeper." We will always try to publish

LOVE STORIES YOU'LL NEVER FORGET
BY AUTHORS YOU'LL ALWAYS REMEMBER

The Editors

To Skip, with love. Seldom does one person mean so much to so many people. And seldom does a person genuinely care about his fellow man. You are an inspiration, a wonderful father, and a grandfather my children can look up to.

One

She was going to die, and there wasn't a damn thing she could do to save herself. She should have stayed in the car. Any idiot would have stayed in the car!

Natalie Courtland heaved an enormous sigh of despair, and her breath left her frozen lips in a wispy gray vapor. The snow swirled around her like a great white twister, blinding and biting as though about to suck her up into the very vortex of the storm and whisk her away. Each step jolted her brutally. She'd shivered so hard and for so long, her bones and muscles ached. Her eyelids were almost frozen closed, her feet and hands stiff and numb. She had fallen so many times as she groped her way through the trees, it was second nature to her now. Somehow she had strayed from the road and seemed to be walking in circles. She didn't know how long she'd been out in the storm. All she was certain about was her own wish to die and be put out of her misery.

Just for a moment Natalie thought she saw light threading through the trees. Was her mind playing tricks on her? If only she hadn't turned off the interstate to look for a gas station. If only she hadn't run into a ditch. If only she hadn't agreed to travel to North Carolina and take part in her friend's wedding. If only she would run into one of those Saint Bernards that patrolled snow-covered areas looking for the stranded. There she was, thinking crazy thoughts again, she realized. Exposure, no doubt. She'd give her gray fox coat to be in front of a warm fire with a steaming cup of coffee in her hands.

She wasn't going to make it to the light, it was too far away, like reaching for a star. Walking was sheer torture. She could hear herself weeping, pleading for help, but it didn't sound like her voice. Her vocal cords felt as though they would split with each cry.

Nick Jordan bolted upright in the kitchen chair for no other reason than he felt something was wrong. He glanced down at his dog, who was cleaning a newborn pup. "You okay, Daisy?" he asked. The setter stopped her maternal ablutions for a second and cocked an ear. She had obviously heard something as well. Nick stood and looked out the window. The snow was coming down fast and hard, at the rate of at least an inch an hour. He'd never seen a blizzard before, but that's not what was making him uneasy. He *sensed* something wasn't right. And he was a man who usually followed his instincts. Instinct alone had saved his life more times than he could remember.

Nick walked to the back door and opened it to get a better look. Who said it never snowed in the South, he thought. Then he heard a noise. Was it the wind? A voice in his head told him to investigate. He pulled a long furry coat from a wall rack and slipped it on. Next, Nick wrapped a muffler around his neck and face, and stuffed his big hands into a pair of brown leather gloves. He glanced back to see that Daisy was okay before letting himself out the back door. He hadn't gone more than a few feet when he realized he'd forgotten his flashlight. He started back for it, but a sound coming from the vicinity of his barn stopped him. Sobbing? The snow crunched beneath his boots as he moved closer.

Natalie picked herself up from where she'd fallen in the snow and tried to brush the white powder from her face. Her vision was blurred; the tears in her eyes had frozen. She stiffened as she heard a noise. Even with the wind howling, she could hear something. She caught movement from the corner of her eye. Damn, if only she could see. With her gloved fists, she wiped at her eyes.

It rounded the barn and stood there, big and furry and horrible. A bear? She swallowed. She would never survive a bear attack. As though advancing in slow motion, the thing moved closer and reached for her. Fear rippled through her body. Natalie's scream pierced the frozen air before darkness engulfed her.

Nick stared at the broken figure lying in the snow. He had seen bodies strewn across battlefields, but for a moment he was more shaken by the vision before him. She looked so fragile, so tenuous against the fierce storm. Without wasting another minute, he swept her up and raced toward the house.

Once inside, Nick threw open the door to a bedroom next to the kitchen and lay her gently on the bed. He shrugged off his heavy coat and tossed it to the floor along with his muffler and gloves. He touched her forehead and cheek, thinking she could have passed as a porcelain figurine. Her fur coat was crusted with ice and snow, her clothes clammy. She was no doubt suffering from hypothermia and perhaps frostbite.

Hell, what did he know about either one? Think, dammit, he told himself.

One thing was sure—he was going to have to get her out of those clothes. First he pulled off the voluminous coat. Each strand of fur had crystallized and weighted the coat down, but it was probably the only thing that had kept her alive. *If* she was alive. Next came the plum jacket she wore, and a multicolored blouse. It was like undressing a limp rag doll. Nick didn't have to be label conscious to know her clothes were expensive. He paused briefly before unbuttoning her skirt, then her slip followed.

Nothing in his years of experience with women

had prepared him for the sight of her underthings. Her bra and panties were a champagne color, made of gossamer. He had never seen material like it before. It was first class and sexy as hell. Her body had been designed for a man, he thought. Suddenly she shivered, and Nick's head snapped up. His gaze collided with a pair of cornflower-blue eyes.

"Who are you?" Her voice was thick and difficult to understand.

"Nick. Nick Jordan. I found you in the snow."

Natalie was vaguely aware that she wasn't wearing anything. At the moment, though, it didn't seem particularly important. She was too tired. "Are you going to rape me?" She'd never be able to defend herself, she knew.

The question caught him totally off guard. The last thing he wanted to do was scare her. He smiled and covered her with a quilt. "No. Not on our first date."

She didn't respond. Her eyelids fluttered closed again. Nick took a deep shaky breath, and trying to remain detached, checked her feet and hands. They were delicate, her toes and fingernails painted a coral shade. As far as he could tell, the color of her skin was close to normal. How she had escaped frostbite was beyond him. At least she looked healthy.

Nick pulled a chair up next to the bed and watched her for a long time, his body rigid with tension. Her breathing was shallow. What if she died? The thought jolted him. He'd seen enough death to last a lifetime. Try for a pulse, he told himself. Surprisingly, he found one right away. That brought a sigh of relief to his lips. "You just might make it after all, pretty lady."

Nick made his way purposefully into the kitchen and pulled out a bottle of Southern Comfort from one of the cabinets. His hands shook. He didn't bother with ice. He splashed a hefty amount into a glass and gulped it.

Natalie slipped in and out of consciousness. At times she heard noises but was too tired to open her eyes to investigate. Nothing else mattered, only that she was warm.

When Natalie finally opened her eyes, her vision was blurred. She blinked and tried to focus her eyes on her surroundings. She was in bed. Sunlight slanted in through a pair of venetian blinds hanging from a window that looked naked without curtains.

Naked?

Natalie peered beneath the covers, and her mouth fell open in surprise. Every stitch of clothing had been removed. Even her bra and panties!

Memories of the previous night came to her slowly, requiring a great deal of concentration. It was like trying to see the events through a murky river. It had been snowing. She distinctly remembered wandering in the snow, her frozen body numb from exposure. Then . . . the bear. Big and ugly and furry, it had reached for her. That was the last image she saw in her mind.

But what was she doing in some bedroom she'd

never seen before? Her gaze darted around the room, taking in the old-fashioned iron bed and simple oak furniture. Her diamond Lucien Piccard watch lay on the night table beside the bed. She spotted two doors, one of which she hoped was a closet containing her clothes.

She pulled the chenille spread off the bed and, sitting up, wrapped it around her body. She stopped to catch her breath. She had never felt so weak. Her legs almost folded beneath her as she climbed from the bed. Grasping the iron frame for support, she waited for a wave of dizziness to pass. The room swayed like a ship set upon a stormy sea. She felt confused, having to stop and think over each move carefully before she made it.

Taking a deep breath, Natalie moved slowly and cautiously toward the set of doors. When she reached the closer of the two, she turned the knob and was surprised to find it turning at the same time in the opposite direction.

Something or someone was out there.

The door was pushed open from the other side, and there it was, that god-awful fur! Still in shock, Natalie covered both eyes with her hands and screamed so loud it echoed off the walls. The bedspread almost slipped off. She couldn't have cared less at the moment that she was stark naked beneath it.

"Dammit to hell, lady, would you stop that infernal screaming!" Nick held both hands to his head. He had one hell of a hangover. When he was able to see past the hammer pounding in his brain, he sucked his breath in sharply at the sight of her near nakedness.

Natalie's head snapped up. Wait, it wasn't a bear at all. It was a man dressed in a big furry coat—the ugliest coat she'd ever seen. Her muscles slackened in relief. Then, much to her mortification, she realized she was half naked and pulled the bedspread tighter around her. She could feel the man's gaze on her as she wrapped the spread around her sarong-style, high enough to cover her breasts.

"Oh, thank goodness you're human," Natalie finally said, her cheeks flushed with embarrassment.

"Who were you expecting, Bigfoot?" he asked, a quizzical expression on his face. Perhaps this was all a part of the confusion and disorientation he'd read about last night when he'd discovered his mother's old medical dictionary stuffed between her cookbooks on a shelf.

Nick couldn't keep from looking at her. There was still plenty of cleavage showing where she had knotted the bedspread. His gaze was drawn to the spot like dry leaves to a flame. He still remembered the oval-shaped birthmark on her inner thigh.

Natalie laughed nervously, still clutching the spread to her breasts. "I had this terrible nightmare last night that I was being attacked by a bear."

He listened, but his eyes were not distracted from viewing the graceful sloping of her shoulders.

"I know it sounds stupid," she muttered. For

some reason he made her acutely aware of the fact she wore nothing beneath the worn chenille spread. She raised her gaze to his. His eyes were brown like his hair, which was streaked with auburn highlights. No wonder he'd looked wild and ominous the night before. The man was well over six feet tall. His shoulders spanned the door frame, and the furry coat made him look twice his size. His chin suggested a stubborn streak, but there was inherent strength in his rugged face. He might not be classified as handsome, but he would certainly turn a girl's head. His mouth was sensual, and the dark stubble on his face gave him a rakish look.

"To tell you the truth," Natalie said, dropping her gaze, "I don't remember much of anything."

"That's because you were delirious and suffering from hypothermia. You scared the hell out of me. How long were you out in that storm?"

She shrugged. "I lost track of the time."

"I thought you were a goner."

"I apologize for any inconvenience I caused," she said. She stuck her hand out hesitantly. "By the way, I'm Natalie Courtland from Atlanta."

"Nick Jordan." He shook her hand but released it quickly. His blood pressure had skyrocketed when the bedspread had slipped and once again partially revealed the perfect body beneath. Not that he hadn't already seen it. But the previous night he'd been more concerned with her life than her figure. Of course, he preferred petite women with long black hair, he reminded himself. Still, this one was quite a looker, despite her short blond hairstyle. She was tall and slender and had one hell of a nice complexion. Her lips looked soft and dewy, like a ripened peach first thing in the morning.

"You're still pale. Hop up on the bed so I can check your feet."

"My feet?" His lengthy stare made Natalie uncomfortable. She had stared down enough people in court, including a judge or two, but it was difficult maintaining eye contact with this man.

He motioned toward the bed, and Natalie did as she was told. Nick pulled off his gloves, unsnapped his coat, and rubbed his hands against his muscular thighs to warm them up. "I just want to make sure you didn't suffer any frostbite traipsing through the woods like Little Red Riding Hood last night."

"I was trying to find help."

"You should never leave your car in the middle of a blizzard." He took one foot in his hand and squeezed it gently. "Can you feel that?" He tried not to stare at the expanse of silky leg attached to the foot he was holding.

She nodded. "My feet and hands feel fine, except they tingle a little." She found herself mesmerized by the size of his hands. They were covered with brown hair and were tough as leather. The calluses at the base of his fingers told her he was used to hard work. Even so, they were gentle and coaxed a multitude of sensations along her inner sole.

"You're lucky to be alive."

"Mr. Jordan—" She retrieved her foot.

"Nick."

"Would you mind telling me where I am, and why I'm uh . . . naked?"

"You're on a peach farm in Cowpens, South Carolina, and you're naked because I undressed you." He said it in a matter-of-fact tone of voice and didn't offer an explanation.

"Oh?" Natalie felt her stomach somersault at the thought of those hands on her body. She fidgeted with the bedspread. The man probably had a perfectly reasonable explanation. Either that or he was a pervert. "Would you mind telling me *why* you undressed me?" She had the feeling he was enjoying her discomfort.

He didn't miss the bright pink flush on her cheeks. He was almost tempted to let her think the worst, but the poor woman had already been through so much. "When I carried you in from the storm, your clothes were wet and frozen." He shrugged. "*Somebody* had to do it," he said, as though he'd made the supreme sacrifice. "But don't worry, I didn't enjoy it. You were unconscious and as cold as an iceberg. When I undress a woman, I want her warm and willing."

Natalie refused to acknowledge his last comment. The man was obviously lacking in manners. But then, considering that he lived in the boondocks, he probably didn't need them, she decided. She painted a smile on her face. "You saved my life, Mr. Jordan. I hope I won't offend you by offering to pay you for your trouble."

Her remark seemed to amuse him, because his

eyes crinkled into tiny webs at the corners. "How much do you figure you're worth?"

She knew he was trying to intimidate her, but she was accustomed to such tactics. It happened in the courtroom every day. She smiled serenely. "I don't suppose one can put a price on one's life," she said, "but I certainly don't want to seem unappreciative. Perhaps there's some other way I can thank you."

"Oh?" Bushy brows bunched together across his wide forehead. This was beginning to get interesting, he thought. "You have anything in mind?"

"Yes," she said, still fidgeting with the bedspread. She was letting him get to her, and it was annoying. Must be those eyes, she thought, and that cocky stance he'd assumed. "I take it you're a peach farmer?"

He nodded.

"Then perhaps there's a piece of machinery you need."

Nick knew a moment of disappointment before it turned to anger. If she thought him a poor struggling farmer, so be it. He'd never put on airs, and he wasn't about to start now with some prima donna from Atlanta. He'd always made it a point to stay away from her kind—but bedding her and liking her were two different things.

"My machinery is just fine, thank you," Nick finally answered curtly. "Besides, I would have done the same for anybody. Unless you can come up with a more interesting offer, you needn't reciprocate."

Her pretense at indifference showed in the look she shot him. It was obvious they came from different worlds. He wasn't bad looking if you liked the rugged outdoors look—which she didn't. Take away that hellish coat, and her secretary would have flipped over him.

"If you're trying to shock me or intimidate me with your language and innuendos, Mr. Jordan, it won't work. I'm a divorce attorney. I've heard and seen it all."

He sighed. "Well, that certainly puts my mind to rest," he said, sarcasm and humor finding a place in his tone. "At least I won't have to worry about toeing the line while we're living together."

Two

Natalie blinked. Living together? Was the man out of his mind? "I'm not staying here," she said as though the mere thought were sheer lunacy. "I have to be in a wedding in Gastonia, North Carolina, tomorrow night. As soon as I can get my car towed from the ditch—"

"Lady, you aren't going anywhere. While you slept much of the day away, the snow has been piling up. The weatherman's calling it the Siberian Express. There are four hundred motorists trapped on I-85, and the governor has declared it a state of emergency." He talked slowly so she could absorb it all in case the hypothermia had dulled her senses. "They've even called in the National Guard. The entire southeast is at a standstill." Nick chuckled at her look of disbelief. "I don't know how you managed to end up this far from civilization, but you couldn't have picked a worse place to get stranded."

Natalie was getting a sick feeling in the pit of her stomach. "When do they expect to have the roads cleared?"

He shrugged. "Well, seeing as how the highway and road officials are working with insufficient equipment and not enough manpower, it could take a couple of days to clear the interstate. But this place is miles from the main roads. It could take a week for the first plow to reach us."

"A week!" Natalie almost shrieked the word. Her desk was piled with motions to be filed with the court, and she had several new clients coming in the following week. "Oh, Lord," she muttered. "What am I going to do?"

When he saw the look of shock and despair cross her face, he shook his head. "Don't you ever watch the news? They've been tracking this storm for days."

"I don't have time to watch television."

Nick couldn't envision her sitting cross-legged on the sofa watching *Wheel of Fortune* either.

Natalie crossed the room and raised a venetian blind to look out, unaware Nick's gaze was trained on her. The bedspread had slipped off her back and barely covered her hips. He took in the way her waist dipped in and flared gently to her hips. "Frankly, I think we should make the best of it," he said.

Natalie's head snapped around. She didn't know what set her teeth on edge most, the smug look on his face indicating he couldn't care less about her plight, the sensual undertone that had crept into his voice, or the way he looked at her as though he could see right through the bedspread. "Exactly what is *that* supposed to mean?" she asked. It was unnerving enough that the man had stripped her naked the night before. He didn't have to make matters worse by flirting. But then, there was no telling when he'd last laid eyes on a flesh-and-blood woman, living out here in the sticks as he did.

When he didn't respond, Natalie went on. "Does anyone else live here with you?" she asked hesitantly.

"Just Daisy and myself." Relief spread over her face. "She's my Irish setter," he added.

"Oh." Natalie's voice was grim.

"Now, I would really appreciate it if you would get back in bed. You're in no condition to be up and around."

"I can't just lie here until the snow melts," she said. "I'll be climbing the walls before long."

Nick raked his hand through his hair and sighed. Whew, had he caught a feisty one! Her dainty chin was thrust out as though ready for a fight. "Look, lady, I've got my own problems, okay? If this weather keeps up, I stand to lose an entire peach crop. So if I seem a little preoccupied—" He dropped the sentence. "As soon as I finish carrying in the wood, I'll get a fire going, and you can lie on the couch. I'll even make you a cup of coffee."

"That would be nice," she said, thinking he wasn't as barbaric as he looked. It wasn't his fault

Greenland had shifted to their doorstep. "Would you happen to have a spare bathrobe I could borrow? I hate walking around draped in this bedspread looking like Cleopatra."

Nick nodded, though he'd prefer seeing her in the bedspread. "You can use my bathrobe if you like." The thought of her naked body tucked in the folds of his bathrobe was a pleasant one.

"Thank you," she said as he disappeared out the door. When he returned, he was carrying a navy blue velour bathrobe.

"Could you tell me where my clothes are?"

"I hung up your dress and fur coat. I washed your other stuff."

Natalie paled. "You mean my . . . uh . . ."

"Your panties, bra, and slip. I never knew what the delicate cycle on the washer meant till I caught a look at your underwear. I figured you'd need them once you woke up. They're hanging over a towel rack in the bathroom. As sheer as they are, I'm sure they're dry by now." He tossed her the bathrobe, and she caught it. "It'll probably be a bit too large, but what the heck." He closed the door behind him on his way out.

Natalie merely stared at the closed door. He had touched her underwear. A perfect stranger had stripped them from her body, then taken it upon himself to wash them. Yes, but they'd been wet and frozen, she told herself. She was still blushing as she slipped on the robe. Large was not the word for it, Natalie discovered. The arms were at least six or eight inches too long, and the hem fell well below her knees. She rolled the sleeves to her wrists and tied the belt securely around her waist. His scent clung to the material like morning dew to a rosebud. She could just imagine his large, hair-rough body wrapped in the garment. She pried her thoughts away from the mental images the scene presented. She had to find a bathroom.

Natalie opened the bedroom door and peeked out into a large, old-fashioned kitchen. Past the kitchen was a comfortable-looking den. She heard a low growl and glanced toward a box against the kitchen wall. An Irish setter gave her a suspicious look from where she lay nursing a litter of new-born puppies.

"It's okay, girl," Natalie said in a soothing voice. "I'm not going to hurt your babies." The dog responded with another low growl. Natalie backed away until she found herself standing next to a bathroom, then quickly made her way inside and closed the door. She tried to lock it but discovered the lock was broken. Did he also have peepholes in the walls? She saw her underwear draped over the towel rack and jerked it off. The man really had some nerve, she decided.

Her reflection in the mirror over the sink brought a frown to her lips. Lord, she was a sight! Most of her makeup had worn off, and her hair was tangled. The shower looked tempting. Perhaps it would make her feel better, she told herself.

Natalie found a towel and washcloth in one of the cabinets. She turned on the faucet in the bathtub and waited until the water was the right temperature before turning on the shower. She disrobed and stepped into the tub, sliding the glass shower door closed. The hot water felt wonderful as it streamed down her body. She shampooed her hair twice, then soaped her body from head to toe. As she stepped beneath the spray of water to rinse, there was the sound of clanging pipes, and all at once the water turned ice cold. Natalie squealed, and in her rush to escape almost slipped in the tub. She grabbed the metal towel rack on the shower door to keep from falling, and her elbow hit the door with enough force to make her curse loudly the person responsible for calling it a funny bone. The entire frame rattled as though it were about to come apart. The door, she learned, was immobile.

Nick banged on the bathroom door as soon as he heard the commotion. Without waiting for a response, he bolted inside. The frosted shower doors hid Natalie from view. "What the hell is going on in here?"

"Please hand me my towel," Natalie said in a strained voice, thankful the doors concealed her. Not that Nick Jordan hadn't already seen every square inch of her body and then some.

Nick grabbed the towel and reached for the sliding door. It wouldn't budge. He shook it. "The door is off the track," he said. "What did you do to it?"

"I tried to keep myself from slipping in the tub," she said, her teeth chattering. "I was showering and all of a sudden the water turned cold."

"If you had waited, I would've warned you about that. You're going to have to turn off the water."

When she didn't respond right away, he called out. "Did you hear me, lady?"

"Yes, dammit, I heard you." Natalie gritted her teeth and forced herself to step beneath the cold water once more to reach the valves. She quickly turned off both. Nick passed a towel overhead. "Thank you," she said as shivers racked her body. She tried to cover herself and get warm at the same time. Goose pimples popped out all over her skin.

Nick, muttering curses under his breath, worked with the errant door for several minutes before he finally got it back on the track. When he slid it open, he stifled the urge to laugh. She looked like a wet mouse standing there, hair dripping on her face.

"Lady, do you always have this much trouble, or have I caught you at a bad time?" She didn't answer, and for a moment all he could do was stare at her. One breast was partially visible despite her attempts to cover herself. The soapy sheen on her body made his mouth go dry.

Natalie fidgeted self-consciously with the towel, but she was too cold to worry about her state of undress. "Could you please . . . uh . . . help me out?" she asked, her teeth chattering. The last thing she wanted to do was slip and go sprawling in the tub in front of him. She held out her hand.

Nick rued the moment he'd found her unconscious in the snow. She could have passed for a centerfold, with the towel doing a poor job hiding what was beneath. Her eyes were vulnerable, her expression embarrassed. It would have been hard to capture that look on film. His jaw was tight as he leaned forward. He ignored the outstretched hand and scooped her easily from the tub.

Natalie felt her stomach do a mad dive. "This wasn't exactly what I had in mind when I asked you to help me," she said, sounding annoyed.

"I was trying to prevent you from falling on your butt," Nick said matter-of-factly. He felt her slick body against his arms. Natalie clutched the towel to her breasts, but he had already burned the memory of the sight of them in his mind. Her short hair curled beguilingly around her face, adding an innocence to her sultry looks.

Her heart thudded against Nick's body, and she sank against him, greedily seeking his heat. The hair on his arms scratched the back of her thighs, spreading a warmth through her that was both pleasant and disturbing. His gaze bore into hers with an intensity that sent the adrenaline gushing through her. She trembled again.

Nick pulled her tighter against him. As crazy as it sounded, he wanted to protect her, comfort her. But he didn't want to stop there. He wanted her. He wanted to touch her all over, taste each inch of flesh he'd bared the night before. He wanted to . . . aw, hell. His mouth came down on hers hungrily. He felt her stiffen in surprise and cursed his own lack of self-control. But he had only to touch her to lose himself, and secretly he had known that all along. He had wanted her the moment he'd first held her in his arms with her pale cheek pressed against his heavy coat.

Nick's lips gentled into a caress against Natalie's. He was on the verge of losing it, but he summoned every bit of restraint he could muster. One hand cupped her face, guiding it to give him better access to her mouth.

Natalie felt his tongue coax its way past her lips, and she was unable to resist granting him access to her mouth. He tasted wonderful. He smelled of the outdoors, of smoke from the fireplace, and of male flesh. The scent was more intoxicating than expensive designer colognes.

Nick broke the kiss, and they both gasped for air. He ran his lips up her throat, amazed how smooth it was. He came to a halt at an earlobe and nibbled it until Natalie shivered again. Her mind suddenly cleared. What was she doing?

Nick's breath was hot on her ear as he whispered into it. "Lady, you sure as hell know how to make a man's blood boil."

"Mr. Jordan—" Her voice sounded controlled despite the things he was doing to her insides.

"Stop calling me Mr. Jordan."

"I'll stop calling you Mr. Jordan when you stop calling me lady. Now, if you'll kindly put me down—"

He ignored her and carried her into the bedroom, dumping her unceremoniously on the bed. "I'll be back with the robe." He disappeared for a moment and returned with the velour garment and her underthings. He sniffed the robe. "It already smells like you. What kind of perfume do you wear?"

She took the robe. "Giorgio."

"Nice."

Natalie waited patiently for him to leave. She felt conspicuous standing there in a towel. But she could be layered in clothing, and the man would be capable of stripping her bare with one look. Those perceptive eyes didn't miss a thing.

"I should have warned you about the water," Nick said, trying to find an excuse to stay a minute longer. "You can't dally in the shower, or it'll douse ice water on you every time. I've been meaning to have it fixed." His gaze zoomed in on her thighs and calves as he spoke, then dropped to her trim ankles and delicate feet.

Natalie had blushed more in the past few hours than she had in her entire life. She was obviously acting loony because her defenses were down from her bout with hypothermia. Otherwise, she would be exercising more control over her thoughts and actions. It was the kiss, too, she reminded herself. That had thrown her off balance. Her insides still churned. Perhaps she was making too much of the kiss, she thought. It *had* been sort of spur-of-the-moment and all. Maybe it would be best if she just pretended it hadn't happened.

"I'd better check the stew," Nick said, knowing it was time to make his exit.

"I want to help," Natalie said, holding the robe in front of her protectively. When it looked as though Nick might protest, she became insistent. "I'm not an invalid, Nick, and I refuse to be waited on. Besides, I'm feeling much better. You'd be surprised how fast I can snap back from a cold or the flu."

She had called him Nick not Mr. Jordan. He

liked the way his name sounded on her lips, nice
and soft and feminine. He wondered how it would
sound whispered in his ear or hot against his lips
in the throes of passion. Damn. "Okay, if you
think you're up to it," he muttered, and disappeared before Natalie had a chance to reply.

Nick made his way into the kitchen, where he
stirred the meat simmering in a large pot on the
stove. He made a fresh pot of coffee, then began
gathering potatoes and carrots and onions to add
to the stew. Natalie entered, wearing his bathrobe, and Daisy gave another low growl.

"Daisy!" Nick admonished the dog, and she lay
her head back down in the box. "Don't mind her,
she's just jittery because of the pups. She'll relax
in a day or two."

"The puppies are cute, from what I can see of
them. Here, let me do that," Natalie said when
she saw he was peeling the vegetables. His pro-
tests went ignored. She washed and dried her
hands and began peeling potatoes. "Have you always lived here alone?" she asked when he took a
seat next to the box and stroked the dog affection-
ately.

"No."

One brow arched on Natalie's forehead, unseen
by Nick. He obviously wasn't a conversationalist.
When the coffee was ready, she poured them each
a cup. "Don't you get tired of all this isolation?"

"I can find company when I need it."

Natalie didn't doubt it for a minute.

"You got a family?" he asked, suspecting she

should notify her husband or boyfriend as to her whereabouts.

"Just my father."

"So you're a divorce lawyer." He looked impressed. "Are you any good?"

The question took her by surprise. "Why? Do you need a good divorce lawyer?" she asked, hoping to draw the man into conversation. He might be used to silence, but her life was filled with noise.

Nick sobered instantly. "No way. I'm a confirmed bachelor if ever there was one. Women are nice to be around, but I wouldn't want to live with one."

"Oh, I see," Natalie said, her voice laced with sarcasm at the derogatory statement he'd just made about her gender. She attacked a carrot, scraping it until none of the peel remained. What was she getting into such a huff about, she wondered. In a few days the snow would melt, and she'd be history in Nick's life. It wasn't going to be easy being confined with him. Nick was still a man and was *somewhat* attractive, she admitted begrudgingly. She might be a no-nonsense lawyer when it came to courtroom procedure, but she was still a woman underneath. Nick Jordan had made her aware of it the minute she'd laid eyes on him.

She was going to have to be very careful.

Nick wondered why Natalie had suddenly stopped talking. Perhaps he'd said too much. Or maybe it was the kiss. His gut warmed at the thought as though he had just taken a swallow of good brandy. She was one hell of a sexy lady. If he thought for an instant that she felt the same about him, he'd haul her into the bedroom so fast, she wouldn't have time to think about it.

Natalie dumped all the vegetables into the pot of stew meat and wiped her hands on a dishtowel. "Well, that's that," she said, glad to be done with the task. At least she wouldn't have to work while Nick stared at her from beneath those thick brown eyelashes. "It'll take several hours to cook."

"What would you like to do until then?" He regretted his words as soon as he'd said them. He had meant them innocently enough, but somehow they had come out sounding entirely different. Silence filled the room. Their gazes met and locked. Trying to clear up the misunderstanding would probably make matters worse.

Natalie felt her stomach lurch at the look in his eyes. What did a man like Nick Jordan usually do in his spare time, she wondered, then pushed the thought from her mind. His look reminded her once more of the kiss they'd shared and how strong his arms and chest had felt when he'd carried her into the bedroom. She could feel the heat of his body drawing her toward him. What was it with this man—this modern-day Paul Bunyan? She had never been attracted to blue-jeans-and-flannel-shirt types. Even on casual outings her dates usually wore expensive slacks and designer shirts. She could just imagine Nick at the Atlanta Athletic Club, but then, most peach farmers probably didn't have time to golf.

He was still watching her with a look of expectancy.

"I think I'll lie down for a while," Natalie finally said, "and let the stew simmer. I guess I'm weaker than I thought." She had become tired from the one small chore, but what she actually needed most was distance from Nick Jordan.

"That sounds like a good idea," he said approvingly. "Before you go, I was wondering if you had any idea where your car is. I assume you have clothes with you."

His question reminded her she had several calls to make. First she had to call her friend in North Carolina and tell her she wasn't going to make it to the wedding. Then she'd have to call her father. She wondered if he was even worried. He'd balked at the storm warning. "Go ahead and go to your friend's wedding. This office will still be standing when you get back. And this time try to catch the bride's bouquet, for goodness' sake. Half your college roommates are on their second marriages, and you haven't celebrated your first."

Marriage was the last thing she needed, she had told herself time and again. After watching so many marriages disintegrate during her years as a divorce lawyer, not to mention her own parents' marriage, she wasn't eager to make the same mistake. Besides, most of her clients were well-to-do and their cases afforded her a nice life-style. Other than an escort now and then, she didn't need a man complicating her life.

"Earth to Natalie. Come in, Natalie."

Natalie blinked. "What?"

Nick studied her. "You looked as though you were on another planet. Should I call a doctor?"

he asked out of courtesy, knowing a doctor would never be able to make it on these roads.

"Oh, no, I'm fine. I was just remembering all the telephone calls I have to make."

He'd bet his bottom dollar one of the calls would be to some fellow named Bobby. She must have called for him a dozen times the night before in her delirium. "We were discussing your car."

She held out both hands. "I have no idea where it is. It must be miles from here. I walked in the snow for hours."

He shook his head. "Well, I'll scout around a bit and see if I can find it."

"I'd appreciate it." The only thing she'd carried with her had been her shoulder bag, and she'd almost left it behind when she'd fallen in the snow the last time. "I'm sure you'd like to have your bathrobe back."

He shrugged. "I don't use it."

"Oh." Her mind ran amok. He probably slept in the nude and traipsed around the house that way when he didn't have company. Oh, Lord, please let her stop thinking of the man's body!

"What kind of car is it?"

"It's a brand new silver Jaguar."

"I should have guessed," he said, rolling his eyes.

Natalie was instantly defensive. "What's that supposed to mean?"

"You just look the type, that's all." He put on his furry coat, wrapped the muffler around his neck, and slipped on his gloves, feeling the hard look she gave him. He hesitated before going out the door. "Uh, listen, go ahead and make the calls you need to make, but I'd appreciate it if you wouldn't answer the telephone while I'm out."

"Any particular reason?"

"I sort of have this girl. Her name's Irma. She's got the temper of a bobcat. If she finds out I've got a good-looking woman staying with me, she's liable to claw my eyes out." With that, he left and closed the door behind him.

Natalie glared at the closed door for several minutes. Irma might not get the chance to claw his eyes out. She would probably beat the woman to it.

Three

Natalie was already up drinking coffee the following morning when Nick stumbled down the stairs wearing only a pair of pajama bottoms. He stopped short when he saw her on the sofa. Beside her sat Daisy, who looked thoroughly content as Natalie stroked her silky ears.

"I didn't hear you get up," Nick said, feeling a bit self-conscious without a shirt. "Did you sleep okay?"

Natalie, in the process of taking a sip of coffee, almost choked. She swallowed painfully. Her gaze froze on Nick's tempting male physique. His chest was broad and powerful, matted with springy brown hair that ran the length of his stomach and circled his navel in a fascinating manner. She realized suddenly that she was staring and pried her gaze away from his body. "I slept very well, thank you," she said in a stilted tone.

Nick merely nodded. Her blond hair curled in disarray around her face. The satin peach-colored robe she wore looked as smooth as her skin.

He'd located her sleek Jaguar the day before, not more than a mile from the house. How the woman had managed to get lost for so long was beyond him. Of course, she had been seriously ill. Her flesh had been cold and blue. Now that her color was back to normal and she seemed to feel well, he ached to hold her again. He was sure her breasts would resemble fine alabaster.

Nick turned abruptly and made his way into the kitchen, where he poured a cup of black coffee. Damn. It wasn't even seven o'clock, and he could feel desire stirring in his loins. He gulped the hot coffee without thinking, and it scalded the roof of his mouth. He muttered a curse. The lady was making him crazy. He should be thinking about his peach crop instead of ogling some woman he'd probably never lay eyes on again once the roads were cleared. The last thing she looked like was a big-city divorce lawyer, he thought. Curled up on the couch as she was, her face still flushed from sleep, she looked as though she belonged in a man's bedroom. *His* bedroom.

"I think I'll take my shower now," Natalie said, startling Nick as she made her way into the kitchen. She caught a glimpse of his wide shoulders and stifled the urge to run her hands over them. He looked as though he could lift a mountain. His biceps bulged from hard work. She knew men who worked out every day to achieve what appeared to come naturally to Nick Jordan. Then she spotted the tattoo on his arm. "What does that tattoo say?" she asked curiously.

"Huh?" Nick turned around slowly, feeling as though he finally had his body under control. His gaze followed the direction of hers to the blue tattoo. "It says Me Lin," he answered simply, realizing how odd the name sounded on his lips after all these years.

"That's a different-sounding name."

"Not when you come from South Vietnam."

Natalie raised her gaze to his face, which was void of expression. "You were in the war?" she asked hesitantly. When he merely nodded, she pressed her mouth into a grim line. "Pretty rotten, huh?"

"Damn right."

Natalie nodded in agreement, then forced a smile. "And this Me Lin. Was she a girlfriend?"

"That's right. *Was.*" He drained the rest of his coffee and poured more.

Natalie knew she had just trespassed on sacred ground. To ease the tension, she laughed. "How come most servicemen come home with tattoos all over their bodies?"

He shot her a disarming grin. "Because the first thing you do when you're granted a pass to town is to get drunk as a skunk and end up at the nearest tattoo parlor. You come out feeling like a real man."

They both smiled. It was difficult to envision him as the young G.I. he must have been before the lines of grief or anger had permanently creased his face.

"Don't forget about the water." It was obvious he wanted to put a halt to the conversation.

"Right. No dawdling." She paused. "By the way, I've already fed Daisy this morning. I found her sitting next to the cabinet where you keep her food. I'm sure her appetite has increased with nursing."

Nick's gaze dropped from Natalie's to her lush breasts, and every muscle in his body tensed. Why did the mere thought of his setter nursing her pups conjure up pictures of Natalie doing the same with his child? In his mind he could see her breasts heavy with milk. He could almost picture a suckling infant in her arms, a miniature fist pressing and kneading her breasts.

He had tried to bury those kinds of thoughts alongside many of his dead buddies a long time before. Why was he digging them up now?

Natalie stared blankly at the man in front of her. What had she said to put that look of despair in his eyes? "Nick . . . are you okay?" She touched his bare arm, and he jumped as though he'd been electrically shocked. He ran a hand through his hair, and Natalie watched the way his chest muscles rippled with the movement.

Nick saw the look of concern on her face. He forced a smile. "I'm fine," he said. "I guess I'm getting cabin fever already. There's no telling how long we're going to be stuck here." The thought scared him. They had shared only one day together. What would happen in three or four? Would he still have his sanity?

Natalie was irritated by the grim look on his face. So, he considered himself stuck with her, did he? Well, he wasn't the only one stuck; she had her own list of responsibilities. Perhaps he was missing Irma, she thought, pressing her lips together peevishly. "Believe me," she said tightly, "nothing would please me more than walking out that front door. I'm not the hermit you are. I prefer civilization." She turned on her heel, stalked toward the bathroom, and slammed the door.

Nick stared at the closed bathroom door. Now, what in tarnation had set her off, he wondered, both brows bunched together at the top of his nose. He pondered the situation. She must be missing her boyfriend, Bobby. The one she'd kept calling for in her sleep. The last thing he wanted to put up with was some woman moping over a man. The more he thought about it, the madder he got. He felt like kicking something. But then, he realized, what the hell business was it of his?

By early afternoon Natalie had thoroughly cleaned the formal living room and dining room of what appeared to be years of dust and cobwebs. Then she went to work on the kitchen. Anything was better than sitting around doing nothing. Nick had disappeared shortly after breakfast, and through the kitchen window she had watched him enter an outbuilding, where he'd been ever since. She had welcomed the time alone. The way he constantly watched her wore on her nerves. She didn't know if he liked her or despised her. Probably the latter of the two, she decided. But what had she done to earn his disfavor, for heaven's sake?

He was a strange man. Natalie was certain there were a number of ghosts haunting his life, and while she felt sympathetic, she didn't want to get involved. In a day or two she would be gone, and Nick Jordan would be out of her life forever.

Natalie washed the white kitchen cabinets until she was sure every bit of dirt and grime had disappeared. She was thankful for the old bib apron she'd found hanging in the pantry. Perhaps it would catch most of the dirt and spare the expensive wool slacks and raw silk blouse she wore. Her stomach growled and reminded her she'd missed lunch, but she was too involved with her cleaning to stop. A package of hamburger meat rested beside the sink, which she planned to use to make chili for dinner.

The back door opened, and Nick stepped in, kicking snow from his boots and shaking it from his thick hair. His presence filled the room. Natalie saw he wore the ugly fur and suppressed a smile. "Do you want a sandwich?" she asked.

Nick openly stared at her as he shrugged out of his coat, recognizing the bib apron that had once belonged to his mother. "What are you doing?"

Natalie beamed proudly. "Cleaning. I got bored sitting around." She paused. "Besides, it's the least I can do to repay you for your hospitality."

Nick tilted his head, gazing at her with uncertainty. The last thing he'd expected to see was Natalie Courtland getting her hands dirty. He walked toward the refrigerator without a word. When he opened it, he stared inside for a full minute before reaching for a jug of milk. It sparkled. "I guess it *has* been a while since I cleaned the place," he confessed.

"Was it before or after Vietnam?" she asked, a teasing lilt in her voice.

They locked gazes briefly and smiled at each other. "No, my parents had the place then. My mother kept it in tip-top condition." He paused. "I sorta let the house go to hell when she died. The only thing I cared about were the orchards." He took a long drink from the jug of milk, screwed the top on, and put it back in the refrigerator. "But you certainly don't have to clean the place out of some sense of obligation. You're welcome to stay as long as you like."

Natalie laughed. "I doubt Irma the tigress would like that very much."

"Bobcat," he corrected. "There's a big difference between a tigress and a bobcat."

"Oh?"

"Sure. A bobcat is wild and easy to strike at the slightest provocation. A tigress"—an enticing smile brought warmth to his eyes and lips—"a tigress is aloof but seductive. She uses all her wiles to catch you, and you go willingly, despite the danger." He gave her a knowing look. "Even so, she can be tamed by the right man." Natalie hadn't the slightest idea what he was talking about, but she listened, mesmerized by the husky timbre of his voice. His expression remained impenetrable.

She clasped her palms together and found them damp with perspiration. Nick had successfully disarmed her this time, but she'd gag herself with the dustcloth before she let him know it. "Why don't you sit down and let me fix you a sandwich? I just made a fresh pot of coffee. I'm sure you could use it after being outside for so long. Aren't you cold out there?"

Nick shook his head as he took a seat at the old maple table that had been in his family for years. He gazed at Natalie from beneath shuttered lids as she prepared his lunch. It had been years since anyone had taken care of a simple need for him, and he felt uncomfortable. Sure, his sister called every now and then from South Dakota to see how he was faring, but she had her own family to contend with.

He had obviously misjudged Natalie Courtland. With her fifty thousand-dollar car and a wardrobe suitable for a princess, he'd thought her a spoiled rich kid. He had suspected a wealthy daddy or a grateful sugar daddy played a part in her life. Now that he realized she earned her own way, he couldn't help but respect and admire her.

It would be interesting to watch her in action in the courtroom, he thought. He had seen her looking fragile and close to death and now in a bib apron looking very domestic, but he'd give anything to see the other side of the lady attorney.

Instinct told him she held her own in the largely male-dominated profession, just as she had put herself on equal footing with him. She would not be easily intimidated—she was too gutsy for that. Still, he didn't want her waiting on him and cleaning his house, though he knew she did it out of some innate need to prove herself capable. The truth was, he didn't want to depend on her. He didn't want to learn to depend on anyone.

Natalie set a ham and cheese sandwich and a bowl of steaming soup in front of Nick. He muttered his thanks as she returned with a cup of coffee. "Is that the new style?" he asked, indicating the apron.

She glanced down and laughed. "It's the absolute rage in Atlanta," she said, pretending to model it for him.

Her movements were fluid and graceful and made Nick's skin itch. "I prefer you in towels," he said, turning his attention to his lunch.

Natalie felt her pulse quicken at the remark. She poured herself a cup of coffee and continued cleaning, although her mind wasn't really on it. Actually, she was flattered that Nick Jordan might find her nice to look at in a bath towel. He had certainly caught *her* eye in his pajama bottoms that morning. If he looked that good from the waist up, she could only imagine how good he looked from the waist down. Her cheeks burned at the thought. Now, what in the world had made her think that? Perhaps it was what happened to people, even strangers, when they were stranded together for any length of time. She was thankful that Nick could get out of the house for a couple of hours—otherwise they'd both go bonkers.

"I have a brother who lives in Atlanta," Nick said without preamble. "He's a bigshot with some investment firm. Makes good money. Goes to all the right places. He's divorced. I could give you his phone number."

Natalie bristled at the suggestion. "I can find my own dates, thank you."

He shrugged. "Sorry, I just thought the two of you might hit it off." And he'd wanted to nip the surprising sense of possessiveness he felt toward her in the bud. It hadn't worked.

Inside Natalie felt hurt that Nick would try to fix her up with another man. Besides, she knew enough bigshots and egomaniacs. Why, she'd even dated one man several times who'd had the audacity to send his chauffeur up to her apartment to fetch her. After the third time she'd sent the driver back with a note to his employer saying that she was going to be busy for the rest of her life. No, the last thing she needed was another bigshot. Unfortunately, they were all she seemed to meet these days.

Natalie saw Nick had drained his coffee cup, and she carried the pot over for a refill. Her hands trembled as she picked up his mug and filled it. As she lowered it, her knee bumped his thigh, and hot coffee sloshed over the side of the mug onto her hand. She made a small sound, and in an instant Nick was beside her.

"You burned yourself," he said, stating the obvious.

"It's fine," she said, wiping her hand on the apron.

"Let me look at it." He took her hand. "I have some salve. It smells like a horse's behind, but it'll do the trick."

"No, really. I'm fine." She withdrew her hand, hurried over to the counter, and set the coffeepot on its burner.

Nick was right on her heels. "You're trembling," he said, his expression anxious. He grasped her shoulders with big hands.

Perhaps she was having a relapse, he thought. She had gotten out of bed much too soon. "I should call a doctor. I should have called one when I found you in the snow," he said guiltily, "but I knew with the blizzard, I'd never get you to the hospital alive."

His face was etched with concern. She looked at him in disbelief. "Why on earth would you call a doctor just because I spilled a little coffee on my hand, for Pete's sake?" The moment was tense. Nick looked as though he had something to say, then thought better of it. She felt like a volcano on the verge of eruption and was afraid to look too closely into his piercing brown eyes. His nearness both disturbed and excited her.

Nick's fingers worked at the knot on the bib apron, and he unwrapped the lengthy ties. "No more housework for you today, Donna Reed. I want your tempting little fanny planted firmly on the couch in front of the fire." He pulled her free of the apron.

Natalie felt a wave of delight rush through her. He found her fanny tempting? Should she confess the fact she found his entire body downright sexy? She stifled the urge to laugh. There was about as much chance of her telling him that as there was of the snow melting in the next hour. Her gaze flitted around the kitchen, refusing to meet his.

"Natalie, look at me." He curved one finger beneath her chin and raised it. When she looked at him, her eyes were guarded, as though she were purposefully trying to keep her feelings to herself.

Natalie tried to relax beneath his encompassing stare, but she failed dismally. In less than two days the man had turned her world upside down. Gone was the confident attorney. She was a vulnerable female who felt branded by his gaze. Heat radiated from his body, filling her with a sense of anticipation.

Nick stroked her jaw. Her skin was smoother than he'd imagined. He hadn't gotten a damn thing accomplished all morning thinking about her. His thumb traced her full bottom lip, and he knew he was going to kiss her—and there wasn't a damn thing either of them could do about it. He captured her face with both hands and held it for a moment, drinking in the loveliness before him. Her expression was cautious as his lips descended.

Natalie felt Nick's mouth cover hers in a kiss that was surprisingly gentle. Her stomach went into a wild spin as he planted one hand against her back and pulled her closer, matching a jigsaw puzzle of planes and curves. She felt weak and confused as his lips became urgent, the way she had when she'd awakened that first morning completely disoriented. Yet, even in her dazed state her body responded. Her arms snaked around his neck, and her mouth became receptive to his. When he sought entry with his tongue, she eagerly parted her lips. He gently massaged her back, and Natalie moaned softly as heat filled her lower belly.

Nick broke the kiss, and they both gasped for air. He showered kisses along her jaw and throat until Natalie was weak-kneed and dreamy-eyed. His hands covered her breasts possessively, and she could feel the heat from his palms burning through her blouse. His fingers kneaded her softness and sent currents of desire through her entire body. She arched against him.

Nick raised his head and looked into her face intently. Her lips were damp and swollen from his kisses. His breathing was ragged, his body ablaze. "This is getting out of hand, lady," he said in a voice so thick, one would have thought he'd been drinking. "We either stop it here and now, or I'm going to carry you into the bedroom and gobble you up."

It sounded so tempting. Natalie already knew what Nick's kisses could do to her. What would it be like to lie naked in his arms and know the power of those thighs, she wondered. "Then what?" Natalie asked. Would Nick make love to her, then forget she existed once the snow melted and she returned to Atlanta? Would Irma reclaim her place in Nick's life and bedroom?

Nick saw the uncertainty in her eyes. "I can't promise you anything, Natalie. Any more than you can make promises to me. Our lives are too different."

She knew he spoke the truth. Still, if she were to let Nick Jordan make love to her, she knew deep in her heart she would want more than a mere romp. She would want commitment, and that just wasn't possible under the circumstances. How had things gotten so far out of control in just two days? "I think we'd better call it quits," she said dully, disentangling herself from him physically if not emotionally.

It took every ounce of willpower Nick possessed to release her. He'd been tempted to lie, promise her anything just to hold her naked in his arms. But he couldn't do it, no matter how much he wanted her. "I'd better take Daisy out," he said, needing to feel the cold air on his face. It would take a fifty-below-zero windchill factor to cool his loins.

"Natalie?" Nick shook her. "Wake up, Natalie." Natalie resisted and snuggled deeper beneath the covers, seeking warmth. Nick shook her again, and through a fog of sleep Natalie heard the urgency in his voice. Her eyelids fluttered open, and she squinted to see in the darkness. What was Nick doing in her bedroom? "What is it?" she asked, wondering why her toes felt so cold.

"You have to get up," he said quickly. "The furnace went out. I can't do anything about it right now. I've got a fire going in the den. We'll have to sleep in front of it."

Natalie blinked, trying to make sense of it all. She had been dreaming about Bobby. His face was still vivid in her mind. "What's wrong with the furnace?" she asked dumbly.

Nick shrugged impatiently. This time he was wearing the top to his pajamas as well as the bottoms. "I don't know. I'll have to get someone to look at it. I don't want to touch the damn thing. It's gas powered. If I screwed up, I could level this house. Come on, before you get chilled."

Natalie climbed from the bed and stumbled out of the bedroom. "It seems all I do these days is try to find a warm place," she muttered in a piqued tone. "I think I'll open a practice in the Bahamas." Not that her father would care. He had planned on Bobby joining his law firm, not her. She had literally begged for a job. The fact that she had made quite a name for herself as a crackerjack divorce lawyer mattered little. Oh, what was the use of going into that now, she asked herself. Just because she was cold and tired didn't give her license to start feeling sorry for herself.

Nick prodded her past the kitchen and into the den, where a roaring fire burned in the fireplace. Natalie moved closer to it. She saw Nick had fashioned a bed out of sleeping bags and blankets.

"Climb under the blankets," he said. "It's very comfortable. I opened three sleeping bags to pad the floor."

"We're going to sleep together?" she asked in a tone that suggested he had purposefully planned some ritualistic orgy behind her back.

"If you want to keep warm, that's exactly what we're going to do. The temperature has dropped another ten degrees and"—he frowned—"would you stop looking at me like that? Right now I'm worried as hell about my peach crop. I don't feel like messing around any more than you do."

Natalie was too cold and sleepy to argue. She knelt down and climbed beneath the blankets with Nick. Much to her surprise, he reached around her waist and pulled her tight against him. "What do you think you're doing?" she asked in outright shock.

"Body heat, lady. Now close your eyes and go back to sleep."

Go back to sleep? she thought. How could any red-blooded female curl up against a man like Nick Jordan and drift off to dreamland?

Nick almost groaned as her pert bottom pressed against his body. His arm curled around her, his hand resting just below one breast. Her satin gown clung to the curves of her body; her perfume did a number on his central nervous system. His peach crop was forgotten for the time being. The fire crackling in the fireplace only enhanced the intimate scene and heightened his desire. He'd give the world to see her naked in the firelight. He felt himself grow hard beneath the blankets.

"Do you *have* to do that?" Natalie said irritably. "It's very disturbing, you know." Disturbing wasn't the word for it, she thought, trying to regulate her breathing.

"Do you have to keep wiggling as if you've got ants in your pants?" Nick finally ground out, unable to control his own blatant desire.

"I was only trying to get comfortable."

"Well, you're creating enough friction to start a forest fire."

Natalie turned over to face him and raised up on one elbow. Nick stifled a groan as one breast threatened to spill out of the bodice of her gown. "You think I'm doing it on purpose?" she asked. She followed Nick's gaze and blushed when she saw half her breast was showing. She tugged on the gown. "You didn't even give me time to put on my robe," she muttered.

Nick rose until his eyes were level with hers. "Look, I know a good way to put an end to all this frustration."

She looked surprised. "Oh?"

His smile was handsome and rakish at the same time. His gaze zoomed in on her lips. "We could get it on right here in front of the fireplace."

Natalie gave a huff, but once again her body betrayed her. It was several seconds before she could speak. "Is that your term for making love, Nick?" she finally asked sarcastically. "I mean, you put it so nicely, so romantically, a girl couldn't help but lose her head."

"Call it what you like, lady, but it all boils down to the same thing, doesn't it? We're hot for each other. Why put ourselves through this misery? Besides, what have you got to lose?"

"My self-respect, that's what. I'm not going to become intimate with some man who has the manners of a goat and hasn't the courtesy to use my name." Natalie paused to catch her breath. "When I sleep with a man, I do it on *my* terms, and there are emotions involved, something you're probably unfamiliar with." She turned her back to him and jerked the blankets over her.

"Well, pardon me for being human, ice princess." Nick turned so that his back faced hers and jerked the covers with equal force. He lay there in the semidarkness for a long time. "There's somebody else, isn't there?"

"That's none of your business."

Nick wasn't about to give up. "Mind telling me who Bobby is?"

Natalie froze beneath the covers. "How do you know about Bobby?" she asked, her tone as cold as the temperature outside.

Nick knew he'd struck a nerve. "You kept calling for him the night I found you. I figured he was your lover. I also figured he was dumb as hell for letting you drive alone in the middle of a snowstorm." When Natalie didn't answer right away, Nick went on. "But then, you haven't tried to call him as far as I know, and he certainly hasn't called here. I was beginning to wonder if you were seeing a married man."

Natalie tried to keep her voice free of emotion. "Bobby was my twin brother," she said so softly Nick had to strain to hear. "He died in a car accident when we were seventeen. I still dream about him when I'm overly tired or not feeling well, so it's no surprise I called for him while I was delirious. Now, if you don't mind, I'd like to get some sleep."

Nick hated himself for what he'd assumed. He wanted to apologize but couldn't find the words. He knew the heartache of losing someone you loved dearly. His father had died while he was fighting in 'Nam, and he was denied permission to come home for the funeral. Some bureaucrat had made provisions for family deaths during a war, but hadn't provided regulations on what to do in the midst of a conflict, and the action in Vietnam had been considered nothing more. Nick pressed his lips together grimly. Funny thing about it, the whole friggin' crusade had resembled war to him, he thought with disgust.

Still, he had handled it like a man.

Losing Me Lin and the baby had been a different matter. He had cried. He still remembered the look in her eyes when he'd boarded the plane for home. His son had had his mother's dark hair and had smelled of soap when Nick had kissed him good-bye. "I'll try to rush through the red tape once I get stateside," he'd promised the small woman with the dark, tearful eyes. "You'll be in the U.S. before you know it." He'd whispered the rest. "Keep the money hidden, and make it last so you and the baby will have plenty to eat. I'll send more as soon as I can."

Not long afterward he received word that Me Lin's village had been destroyed during the fall of Saigon. Me Lin and their son were among the murdered. His world had come crashing down around him.

Nick heard Natalie make a sound in her sleep. He had been wrapped up in his own pain for so long, he had forgotten other people suffered as well. Irma's skillful hands had soothed him over the years, but they both knew nothing would ever come of the relationship.

Who kissed away the hurt for Natalie Courtland, he wondered. It scared him that it mattered so much. He had learned the hard way that caring for people meant taking chances. He would chance anything in the world but his heart.

Four

Natalie opened her eyes the following morning and found herself cocooned tightly in the warmth of Nick's arms. His gentle snore told her he was still sleeping, and she used the opportunity to free herself from his clutches.

Nick opened his eyes and hesitantly released her. The smile on his face was as sexy as his brown sleep-filled eyes and mussed hair. He looked amused. "You were wonderful last night, darling. Was it good for you too?"

Natalie shot him a withering glance. "Keep dreaming, mister," she said dully, and climbed from beneath the blankets. A shiver racked her body. "It's freeeezing!"

"It's warm under the blankets," Nick replied smugly, his gaze zooming in on her erect nipples. Static electricity molded her gown to every curve, clinging sensually to her thighs and calves in a way that took his breath away. The person responsible for designing the gown must have been a lusty soul, he thought. Damn, he was already hard, and he hadn't been awake five minutes.

Natalie plucked the gown from her body without success. She would have to put on her robe. "I have to have a cup of coffee the minute I wake up," she explained, and started for the kitchen, unnerved at the way Nick's eyes traced the lines of her body. She hurried into the bedroom she'd been using and grabbed her robe. After slipping into it, she tied the satin belt around her waist securely and stuffed her feet into matching slippers.

"Okay, get back under the blankets, and I'll make the coffee," Nick grumbled once she'd returned to the kitchen. He was already climbing out from under the bed covers and cursing the temperature. When Natalie merely stood there, he pointed to the makeshift bed. "You heard me. The last thing you need to do is get chilled. Now, scoot."

Natalie did as she was told without arguing. Kicking off her slippers, she climbed in Nick's side of the bed, where it was still deliciously warm, and pulled the covers to her chin. His masculine scent clung to the sheets. Nick, she noticed, trying not to laugh, had slipped on his fur coat. His feet were bare. She swallowed a giggle as she watched him tiptoe across the kitchen floor as though it were scattered with thumbtacks. The linoleum probably felt like ice beneath his bare feet.

"As soon as I've finished making coffee, I'll get a fire going," he said in a shivering voice. "I got up twice during the night to add more wood, but it must've burned out." He wasn't about to confess the fact that he'd gazed at her for a long time as the flames flickered and painted shadows on her lovely face.

All that remained of the fire now were a few red embers putting out very little heat. Natalie was thankful Nick had carried in a load of wood the night before. At least he wouldn't have to battle the bitter cold outside. Daisy and her pups had been moved closer to the hearth, and the noises coming from the box told Natalie it must be breakfast time. She could hear the puppies grunting and wiggling as each tried to claim an engorged nipple. The thought brought a smile to her lips, and she snuggled deeper under the covers and closed her eyes lazily.

"Am I supposed to drink it for you too?"

Natalie opened her eyes and found Nick standing over her with two steaming mugs. She sat up immediately. "God bless you," she said, reaching for one of the cups. Nick set his cup aside and stacked several thick logs in the fireplace. In just a matter of minutes the flames were licking the wood, setting it ablaze. Shrugging off his coat, he climbed in on Natalie's side of the bed.

"You could have at least kept it warm for me," he mumbled.

The coffee was strong and hot, and Natalie sipped cautiously. "What are we going to do?" she finally asked.

Nick looked up. "About what?"

"The furnace, for heaven's sake!"

"Oh, that. I suppose we'll have to dress warm today."

She sighed at the thought of spending the day in a room that resembled a freezer. "You mean you're not going to try to get someone to fix it?"

"Who? Santa Claus? He's the only one I know with a sleigh."

"Isn't there *somebody* you can call?" she asked in disbelief.

"Oh, there are plenty of people I can call, but how they're going to get out here is another thing. Have I told you we just suffered through a record-breaking blizzard? In fact, I heard on the news last night that it hasn't snowed this much since 1939."

Natalie wasn't in the mood for statistics. "We can't just lie in bed all day."

"We could if you'd cooperate."

"Stop making wisecracks, this is serious. We could die." When his look turned doubtful, she became persistent. "What if we run out of food? Or wood for the fireplace?"

He took a sip of his coffee. "What if my entire peach crop freezes?"

"Is that all you can think about right now? Your blasted peach crop?" Natalie didn't realize her voice had risen. "I'm talking life and death here."

Nick was mesmerized by the rise and fall of her breasts, and the tiny nodes that strained against the fabric of her robe. His thoughts ran wild while she sipped her coffee and gazed into the crackling fire as though trying to figure a way out of their dilemma. "I'm not going to let anything happen to you, Natalie," he said gently. "Hell, I've been in worse situations than this. Why, I remember once in 'Nam—"

"Don't tell me," she said through gritted teeth. "I'm a woman, not a guerrilla fighter."

His face broke into a leisurely smile that sent her pulses racing. "So I've noticed. But I think you underestimate yourself. Perhaps you're stronger than you think. I'll loan you a couple of sweaters . . . we'll keep warm."

Natalie finished her coffee in silence. Why was she blaming each mishap on Nick? It wasn't his fault the furnace was broken. And she didn't want him to try to repair it himself if it was dangerous. "I didn't mean to snap," she apologized. "I'm going stir crazy."

Nick seemed to ponder her words over the rim of his coffee cup. "Tell you what. This afternoon we'll try to take a walk." When Natalie looked at him as though she thought he'd lost his mind, he went on. "It's colder in here than it is outside. I'll loan you a pair of boots. In the meantime we'll drink coffee until the place warms up a bit. I can see now we're going to have to close off some rooms in order to keep this part of the house warm. From now on we'll be living in the kitchen and the den. Of course, there's a small heater in the bathroom. We'll manage well enough. Just keep telling yourself it's temporary."

Did that mean they would continue to share the same bed, Natalie wondered. If they kept living in such close quarters, something was bound to happen. She glanced at Nick. She would have given anything to know what he was thinking. He had a ruggedness and strength that attracted her feminine side, but common sense told her they were too different to even entertain the idea of a relationship. Darn the man! He knew what he was doing to her, and he was enjoying every moment of it. It wouldn't surprise her if he had purposely shut off the furnace to get her into bed with him. She didn't trust Nick Jordan one bit.

As though reading Natalie's thoughts, Nick reached out and stroked her cheek sensuously. The personal contact made her shiver. He looked concerned. "Cold?"

"N-no." Anxiously she ran her hands through her short hair, trying to ignore the profile of his face. The night's growth of beard made him look sexy. Did he realize she was attracted to him despite her attempts not to reveal it? She sighed inaudibly. This was no time to get romantically involved with a man. She had duties and responsibilities waiting in Atlanta. The sooner she got back there the better.

Nick watched the play of emotions on her face and wondered what she was thinking. There was a battle raging inside her head, and he knew it. Instinct told him it concerned him. Without warning, he took her empty coffee cup and set it aside. The action made her glance at him in surprise, and he used the movement to his advantage. First he kissed the tip of her nose, ignoring the gasp that escaped her lips. When she closed her eyes, he kissed the fluttering lids softly before his mouth descended to hers.

His warm lips surprised her at first, but as Nick coaxed her, Natalie felt herself responding. He eased her down gently onto her back, and his mouth roused her passion, sending currents of desire through her. Eagerly Natalie's lips parted to receive his searching tongue. One of his hands reached beneath the blankets and cupped a breast, fingering a nipple until it was tight and quivering. He broke the kiss and pressed his lips against her throat, skimming downward to the top of her nightgown.

When Natalie felt his lips on her breasts, she almost crooned in delight. The fabric grew damp under his demanding mouth and chafed her nipples, tantalizing each bud even more. Heat radiated through her body, low in her belly, between her thighs. Nick seemed to know all her pleasure points, all that delighted her. Her arms curled around his neck, and once again their lips meshed. Her body arched intimately against his. What was this insane power he exerted over her?

Natalie felt like a drowning woman. Slowly, as Nick worked his magic, kissing the valley between her breasts, tonguing her navel until she squirmed against him, her thoughts tried to surface. What was she doing? Her mind attempted to rationalize what her body couldn't. She was kissing the man who'd saved her life. She was a mature woman, she wasn't ignorant of sex. Then her mind rebelled. She didn't want mere sex with Nick Jordan, she wanted more. More than Nick would ever be capable of offering.

After all, he had Irma. No strings attached. What more could a man ask for?

Nick felt Natalie's body stiffen. One minute she was warm and pliant in his arms, and the next moment she felt like a statue. He broke the kiss and stared into her blue eyes. He regarded her quizzically, but she turned away, her composure as fragile as fine crystal at the moment. After a moment their breathing slowed and became normal.

Nick tried to figure out the closed expression on her face. Hadn't she responded to his every touch? Her body was well tuned to his. She was like a musical instrument, perhaps a flute or harp. He knew he could coax beautiful sounds from her. "Did I do something wrong?" he finally asked, feeling as clumsy as he had as a youth in high school.

"You did nothing wrong. It's me."

Nick leaned up on one elbow and studied her face intently. "Want to tell me about it?"

She didn't have to stop and think about her answer. "No."

Nick's disappointment quickly turned to confused anger. "Fine," he said abruptly, climbing out from beneath the covers. It was obvious he'd become excited during the early stages of their lovemaking, and Natalie felt guilty for calling things to an abrupt halt. "I'll get the coffee this time," she said.

By mid-afternoon the sun was shining, making the snow blinding to the eye. Natalie could barely walk for all the clothes she wore. Beside her, Nick was wearing his familiar coat. He had rolled up a pair of socks and stuffed one into each toe of a pair of boots to make them fit her. The boots almost reached her knees. "I'm waddling like a duck," she said, trying to talk through the thick scarf around her face. The whole idea of wrapping herself like a mummy to walk in knee-deep snow had sounded absurd. But it had become claustrophobic in the house.

"Yes, you are," Nick acknowledged. "Now you know how a pregnant woman feels during the last couple of months."

"I'm going to remain childless," she said with determination.

"Oh, I don't know. You'd make a good mother. And half the fun of being pregnant is getting there." There was a flicker of amusement in his eyes.

Natalie was thankful he didn't see the bright flush on her cheeks. "Nothing is sacred with you, Nick Jordan."

He stopped abruptly and turned to her. One cheek was barely visible, and not even the fleshy color of his blue-ribbon peaches could compare to it. He touched it lightly, tentatively. "Some things are."

Natalie was caught off guard. The moment stretched out uncomfortably. She backed away, and his hand fell to his side. "Anyway, what do *you* know about being pregnant?" she asked, trying to keep the conversation light.

"Probably more than you think."

"Is that your way of telling me you've fathered half the county?"

He threw his head back and laughed, and a wispy vapor escaped his lips. "No, dear. I'm a cautious man."

Natalie stopped walking and gazed at the untouched countryside. Limbs sagged beneath the weight of the snow. "It's beautiful," she said. Past the outbuildings she could see where the orchard began. It seemed to go on for miles. "How much land do you own?"

He was vague. "Enough to see a profit if the crop doesn't freeze."

She looked concerned. "Do you think it will?"

"I don't know. It will if the temperature keeps dropping. But I plant a high-quality grade. The peaches are fairly hardy. There's a lot to know about growing peaches—chill factors, diseases, you name it." They walked in silence for a while. "The weather report sounded good this morning. It's supposed to warm up."

"Really?" Natalie looked hopeful.

Nick had purposefully put off telling her. He knew she wanted to get back to her high-society life in Atlanta, and it irritated him. "Not by much," he said, "so don't run in and start packing yet. The roads are still impassable." What would she tell her friends about him when she returned home, he wondered. Would she compare him to Li'l Abner in the comic strip?

"That's a good sign, isn't it? Is there a chance the temperature will warm up enough to melt the snow?"

"Not right away. I don't think you'll get out of here until the plows find us. They've cleared most of the interstate." He had watched the news while she'd showered.

When Natalie shivered, Nick decided it was time to go back inside. Although she would have preferred doing a little more sight-seeing, common sense told her she should get warm. Several hours later, though, she was bored.

"Isn't there *something* I can do?" she asked hopefully. "Scrub the wax build-up off your floors or wash the woodwork?"

Nick had a great idea. She could strip down to nothing, and . . . Common sense told him not to voice his thought. He could just imagine her branding him with the fire poker and ending his sex life forever. He sighed heavily. He couldn't remember a more frustrating time in his life.

"No, Hazel," he said dully. "My floors and woodwork are fine. As you've probably observed, I don't expect my house to be squeaky clean. Now, why don't you relax? In a couple of days you'll be back at work wishing you had some free time on your hands." He decided he liked her in his sweaters, even if they did swallow her up. "I have a couple of games I keep around just for blizzards," he offered.

"I'll just bet you do," she said with a snort.

He rolled his eyes. "I'm serious. Would you like to play one?"

She looked doubtful. "Do you have Monopoly?"

He frowned. "Why, are you especially good at it?"

"I can hold my own."

Nick pulled himself off the sofa and went into another room in the house, where several games were stacked on a shelf in a closet. He grabbed the Monopoly game and dusted the front of the box. There was no telling how long it had sat in that closet. It probably hadn't been touched since his parents died. When he returned, he found Natalie in the kitchen.

"Tell you what," she said, "you set up the game, and I'll make us each a cup of hot chocolate."

Nick nodded and set the game up on the floor in front of the fireplace, where the bed covers had been folded and stacked in a corner. It was warm and cozy and inviting. It represented coziness in its simplest form. Natalie had brought the feeling in with her the night of the snowstorm, only she'd been too sick and he too worried to notice. The feeling frightened him. He didn't want to get used to these kinds of evenings then have to let go in the end.

"What do you want to be?" he called out as he set up the board.

"Pardon?"

"Which game piece you want to be? A dog, a car, an iron, or a belly dancer?" he asked, grinning as his mind did an instant replay of his former naughty thoughts.

She frowned at him from the kitchen. "There's no such piece." She shrugged. "I'll be the dog." At the mention of the word, Nick automatically glanced over at Daisy, who was napping with her pups. He had already taken her out twice, giving Natalie a chance to hold each puppy. Once he'd returned, she had announced she was taking them all home with her. Nick doubted seriously that Daisy would let her get as far as the back door.

Natalie carried in two steaming mugs of hot chocolate. She set them down on the floor, then sat cross-legged facing Nick. "Okay, who goes first?"

Nick gazed at her thoughtfully. "You know, I would never have imagined you sitting in the middle of the floor playing Monopoly. Come to think of it, you don't look like the chili and beef stew type either."

For some reason his opinion meant a lot to her. "What type do I look like?" she finally asked.

He shrugged. "At first I thought you were a spoiled brat and that you'd bitch constantly about our situation."

She blushed. "Well, I'll admit I've complained—"

"Anybody would under the circumstances. But you've more or less taken everything in stride. A real trouper," he added.

"Thank you. And you've been a considerate host."

"Does that mean you'll sleep with me tonight?" he asked hopefully, cocking his head to the side and grinning like a big kid.

"No." Her face burned, knowing he wasn't merely referring to sharing his sleeping bags. "Now, are we going to play Monopoly or not?"

"Why couldn't I have gotten stranded with a wanton woman?" Nick muttered. "Instead of some Doris Day clone."

Two hours later he leaned back. "I'm broke."

Natalie paid him no heed. "That's tough. You landed on Boardwalk, and I have three hotels. Let's see, you owe me—"

"You've got all the money. How am I supposed to pay, for heaven's sake?"

"Are you quitting?"

"I don't have much choice, do I?"

"No, you really don't."

"I bet you're hell in court," he said speculatively. "A real tigress. What made you decide to become a divorce lawyer?"

She shrugged and started picking up the game pieces. "My father is a lawyer. Bobby and I planned from the time we were children to go into law. Except Bobby wanted to be a criminal lawyer. We both thought it would be exciting."

Nick saw the flash of pain in her eyes. It lasted only a second before it disappeared. He wondered briefly if losing Bobby had affected her relationships with other people, especially men. He was almost sure it had. He had recognized her "arm's-length" attitude right away. But what about her father? Surely he offered her the emotional support she needed.

"I know this probably sounds stupid, but I think I chose divorce law to sort of get back at my mother."

"What did she do?"

"She walked out on us." Natalie tried to sound indifferent. "Bobby and I were only eight years old at the time. After that my father called in his unmarried sister to care for us. We called her 'prune-face' behind her back because she was always pursing her lips in disapproval. Anyway, I guess Bobby and I grew extra close because of it all."

"Do you hate your mother?"

Natalie thought about it. "I used to. But then I realized I wouldn't want to be married to my father either." She laughed and put the lid on the Monopoly box.

Nick shoved it out of the way and without warning pulled Natalie onto his lap. Her squeal of protest didn't hinder him in the least. "Be still," he ordered. "I only want to hold you."

Those words seemed to ease her mind, because she stopped struggling. In fact, after a few minutes she lay her head on his shoulder. The smell of his aftershave was nice, and his sweater felt good against her cheek. Neither spoke for a long time but merely watched the fire lap hungrily at the logs.

"What are you thinking, Natalie?" His voice startled her in the quiet of the room.

"I'm thinking what a nice man you are." She swiveled around in his arms so that she was facing him. "I mean, I know we're different and all, but being with you these three days has shown me a side of life I never imagined."

Nick couldn't help but reach out and trace the delicate line of her jaw. "And what is your life like?"

She shrugged. "It's nice, I suppose. I live in a high-rise condo. Very chic, as my decorator says." She laughed. "I'm not home much, though."

"A lot of dates?" He was surprised how much that thought bothered him.

"No, I work late most nights. The phone isn't ringing off the hook after hours, and I can work undisturbed. Then I go home, pop a frozen dinner in the oven, eat, and go to bed." She smiled. "Pretty exciting stuff, huh?"

Nick chuckled. "I see that I've finally met someone in the fast lane." His thumb traced her bottom lip. "You know I'm going to kiss you," he said matter-of-factly.

"And your enormous ego tells you I'm not going to make one move to stop you."

He was smiling as his lips captured hers. He'd been wanting to kiss and make love to her for what seemed like an eternity, but for some reason it had become important to get to know her before he rushed in and took what he wanted as he usually did. In three days he had learned a lot about her, which made the kiss even sweeter. His tongue slipped past her lips and sought the delights within. His arms tightened around her.

Natalie leaned against him, feeling the strength in his arms and chest. His lips never stilled. His tongue traced her bow-shaped mouth, then he took her bottom lip between his teeth. Natalie shivered with pleasure. One hand slipped beneath the bundle of sweaters she wore and cupped a breast, then teased the nipple through the lace cup. Natalie felt her head spin. Low in her belly, a delightful warmth began to spread.

Nick reached for her hand and pressed it against the front of his jeans, where his arousal was more than noticeable. Natalie sucked in her breath at the intimate gesture. When Nick broke the kiss, they were both gasping for air.

"See what you do to me?" he asked, his voice

thick, his eyes glazed with passion. "I want you, Natalie."

"Nick—"

"We're not children. You know damn well we'll be sharing a bed in front of the fireplace tonight. Do you think I'm made of stone?"

"It's too soon."

"Who says?"

"Like you said, we've known each other for only three days."

"I know all I need to know about you." When she started to protest, he put a finger against her lips. "What are you afraid of?"

Natalie took a deep breath. He looked as though he were prepared to wait her out. "The truth? You want me to tell you the God's honest truth?" He nodded, a strange look in his eyes. "I'm afraid if we make love, I'll fall in love with you," she confessed.

He couldn't believe his ears. It took several minutes before he could speak. "Would that be so bad?"

"For me it would. Unless you're planning to uproot all your peach trees and move them to Atlanta."

"You could move your practice," he said simply.

"To Cowpens?" Natalie pulled herself up from his lap. "I don't believe we're even discussing this. We barely know each other. You could be mentally deranged for all I know."

"There's one way to find out."

"How?"

"You'll have to get naked and lie in my arms."

Natalie felt the sting of tears. "That's not funny."

Nick reached for her, but she escaped him. "You're crying," he said in disbelief. "I make a pass at you, and you cry? Forget I said anything, okay? I wouldn't have your body on a silver platter. Feel better?" He reached out and caught a tear on his fingertip. Without saying a word he pulled her into his arms and held her. "I didn't mean to make you cry," he said gently. "It's just that you're so lovely, it's hard to concentrate on anything else."

Natalie sniffed. "Oh, Nick, I'm such a fool for crying. It's only . . ."

"What?" He pulled back and looked into her eyes.

She swiped at a tear. "It's only that everybody I've ever cared about . . . well, I've lost them. I just don't think I can handle any more pain."

Nick studied her a long time before letting her go. When he spoke, his voice was harsh. "You haven't exactly cornered the market on broken hearts, lady."

Five

"What is *that* supposed to mean?" Natalie demanded, feeling shattered that he should make light of what she'd told him.

"It means you don't have to spend the rest of your life licking your wounds and feeling sorry for yourself."

Natalie felt her face burn in anger. For a moment all she could do was stare in disbelief. When she spoke, her words were controlled. "Are you talking about me or yourself, Nick?"

Nick stood and rammed his hands in the pockets of his jeans. He faced the fireplace and was almost hypnotized after a moment of staring into the flames. What he'd told Natalie about herself really applied to him, and he knew it. After all these years he was still licking the wounds that had literally torn his guts out more than a decade earlier. And yes, he felt sorry for himself at times.

He'd become embittered. He cursed himself mentally for not being stronger. And he cursed Natalie for being able to read him so easily.

"Nick?"

"Huh?" He looked up and found Natalie watching him in an odd way.

"I'm sorry. All we do is fight. I know you'll be thankful to see me gone."

The thought jolted him to the soles of his feet. Natalie gone? His mind refused to accept it at first. "No, I've enjoyed your company. I would have gone nuts stuck here with no one to talk to." He was silent for a moment. "Maybe I'll call you sometime when you get back to Atlanta. Just to see how you are," he added quickly, knowing it would be best not to.

"That would be nice," she said, certain he wouldn't.

He'd go crazy not seeing her. "Atlanta's not far from here. I could make the drive in a couple of hours."

Natalie's heart leapt with joy. Nick wanted to see her again. Her smile faded. Of course, he was probably trying to be polite. Once gone, she was sure she would never see him again. Irma would come back and claim her rightful place in Nick's life, and Natalie would be but a flicker of a memory.

For some odd reason Natalie didn't resent Irma. Nick had probably been able to tell her about his life in Vietnam. If Irma had been able to erase just one ugly memory, Natalie was grateful, because she could look in Nick's eyes and see ghosts.

"Unless you'd rather I didn't," he said, taking her silence as a way of rebuttal.

"Sure you can visit." She tried to sound enthusiastic, but it reminded her of the holiday seasons in college—close friends promising to visit or call while they were away but never doing it. Natalie had learned not to count on it. Face it, she told herself. She was never going to see him again once she left. A lump filled her throat that made swallowing impossible.

"Hungry?" Nick glanced at the clock.

"A little, I suppose." Her mind wasn't really on food, but she knew Nick was perceptive. He would notice something was wrong immediately and question her. It was impossible to lie to the man— he'd get it out of her. He had probably been in charge of interrogating prisoners in Vietnam.

"I thought it would be nice to grill steaks in the fireplace tonight," he said. "I do it all the time in the winter."

With whom, she wanted to ask but didn't. "I'll put a couple of baking potatoes in the oven," she said, already pulling herself to a standing position. "And I'll make a salad."

In thirty minutes time Natalie had scrubbed the baking potatoes, pricked them with a fork, and buttered them. Before sticking them in a shallow pan, she sprinkled seasoning salt all over them. Next, she washed the salad greens and left them to dry on a paper towel. When she turned around, she saw Nick opening a bottle of wine.

"I see we're going all out tonight," Natalie said, amused.

He grinned, something he did sparingly. "I plan to ply you with this stuff and seduce you. It always works in the movies."

"Well, this isn't Hollywood, and I seldom drink. When I do, I know my limits."

Nick looked at her as though she'd just dropped a bomb in his lap. "You know, you are one hell of a fun lady to be stranded with," he said. Nevertheless, he handed her a glass of burgundy after he'd given it time to breathe. He held a glass as well as he leaned on the counter and watched her prepare the salad. She stopped several times to take a sip of her wine.

"It's good," she acknowledged.

"So what do you do for fun, Natalie Courtland?"

"Oh, I like to read and cross-stitch. Sometimes I go to a movie with a friend. And I just started golf lessons. I have a lot of interests but no time," she added glumly.

Wine spewed from Nick's mouth as he burst into laughter. "I'm sorry," he said as Natalie looked up in surprise. "I just thought maybe there was a wild side to you, but I can see our little adventure here isn't going to be like one of those fun-ship cruises."

She shot him an indignant look. "It just so happens I live a very full life, Nick Jordan. If you think I spend my time in singles' bars looking for fresh meat, you're wrong. So if I bore you, that's tough." Natalie took a long sip of her drink, knowing that Nick was watching. One or two droplets landed on her bottom lip, and she licked them with her tongue.

She could never bore him, he thought. "I'll bet you made straight A's in school," he said. "Honor roll?"

She faced him squarely. "Yes, as a matter of fact, I did. I graduated from college with honors, and I graduated second from the top of my law school class. Satisfied? I knew exactly what I wanted to do with my life." She picked up her wineglass, and her hands trembled. Why she felt she needed Nick's approval was beyond her. She was far better off than he, isolated as he was in a dusty old house miles from nowhere.

Nick sipped his wine quietly. "I can't believe you don't plan on having children," he said, changing the subject entirely. "Like I said earlier, you'd make a wonderful mother. Why deny yourself that pleasure?"

"That should be obvious," she said on a laugh. "For one, I'm not married nor do I intend to marry, and two, I'd probably be one of those overprotective mothers. I'd be terrified something bad would happen to the baby."

"Like with Bobby?"

He *was* perceptive. She lowered her lashes. "Yes, like Bobby. Then I'd have to face being alone again." She drained her glass and refused a refill. One glass of wine had her thinking and feeling things that made her uncomfortable. It made her say things that were better left unsaid.

"What about your father?"

"He and I don't have a relationship. Not a close one anyway. He changed after my mother left.

Sort of withdrew from Bobby and me. I guess that's why Bobby and I grew so close." She laughed. "When we were in high school, the teachers saw to it that Bobby and I weren't put in the same classes. We pulled more pranks."

"You said he was seventeen when he was killed?" Nick said gently, trying to draw information from her. She seemed to keep so many things under lock and key.

There was a flicker of pain in Natalie's eyes before she answered. "Yes. Bobby and I did everything together. We had the same interests, the same friends. We even double-dated. Old 'prune-face' "—she paused—"that was our aunt Meg who came to stay with us and whom we later renamed Attila, didn't think my brother and I had a healthy relationship. I don't know if the woman was perverted or just hated to see Bobby and me happy." She took a deep breath. "I was supposed to go with Bobby and our friends to a drive-in movie the night he died, but I had the flu. My dad didn't tell me until the next morning." The silence stretched between them. "I guess that's when I really became determined to go to law school. Although Bobby and I had planned to go together, I secretly felt intimidated. There weren't as many women enrolled back then. But later I felt that if I could survive the loss of my twin, I could handle anything." She smiled and held up her empty glass. "See what one glass of wine does to me? I spill my guts."

Nick laughed. "I was hoping for another kind of

reaction." Inside, though, he was thankful she had confided in him. At least now he felt he knew part of what made Natalie Courtland tick.

Natalie could tell he was teasing. She seriously doubted Nick Jordan was the type to get a woman drunk and take advantage of her. Of course, there was always room for error. She shoved her wine-glass away.

Nick went to the refrigerator and pulled out two steaks that had been marinating. He disappeared in the vicinity of the garage and returned holding the metal piece that fit inside his grill. After arranging it carefully over the logs in the fireplace, he returned to the kitchen for the steaks. "How do you like yours cooked?"

Natalie looked up from wiping down the counter. "Medium rare, please." While he carried the steaks to the grill, Natalie began setting the table.

When Nick returned, he saw the table had been set correctly and tastefully. "That's something I never do."

"What?" Natalie glanced over her shoulder from where she was standing at the sink.

"I never go to the trouble of setting a table. I just cook it and eat it—usually in front of the television set with Daisy begging at my feet." He felt a stab of regret that he'd no doubt go back to his old ways after she left.

When the steaks were ready, Nick set them aside on the grate to keep warm until the potatoes were finished baking. He poured himself another glass of wine. "Want some more?" he asked Natalie, his eyes challenging her.

"No thanks."

"Afraid you'll lose your inhibitions and turn into a wild woman?" he asked, a teasing lilt in his voice. He sat at the counter and studied her. "I'll bet you're one hell of a passionate woman when somebody pushes the right buttons."

"I don't think that's any of your business."

"Aw, c'mon, Natalie. We've been living under the same roof for three days. Surely you've grown a little fond of me in that length of time."

If only he knew. She was growing more than fond, and that's what scared her. And speaking of buttons, she was certain Nick Jordan knew which ones to push. Natalie busied herself at the sink rinsing dishes. Before she knew what was happening, Nick came up behind her and slipped his arms around her waist. He pressed warm lips to the nape of her neck. "I want you," he said simply.

"You've had too much wine." She tried to pull away, but it was hopeless.

"That's because I'm trying to numb all my senses," he said, his lips inching their way up to her earlobe. Natalie shivered, and he laughed, the sound a low, sexy chuckle in his chest. "What's a man to do? You go sashaying about in gowns that would tempt a man hell-bent on celibacy."

She laughed. "You don't even know the meaning of the word."

"And you wear that perfume that drives me wild."

"Nick—"

He turned her around and took her in his arms. "I want you, Natalie Courtland. I'm going to have you. Take this as a warning, because there's nothing either of us can do to stop it." His mouth came down on hers, hard and demanding, his tongue foraging past her lips.

Natalie was stupefied. His hands roamed over her freely, crushing his body against hers. Escape was impossible. Her hips were pressed against a cabinet door. The kiss deepened, sweeping her thoughts away with it. Once again her body responded with an urgency that was both pleasurable and uncomfortable. After Nick broke the kiss, his lips skimmed her forehead, her eyelids, her temples, leaving her flesh hot in their wake.

He buried his head between her breasts, inhaling her essence. Her scent was implanted in his brain and often spilled over into his dreams.

Natalie was literally gasping for air, and her knees threatened to buckle beneath her. She was fighting, fighting for survival. Nick was breaking down all her defenses one by one, so she felt helpless in his arms. At that moment he possessed the power to do with her as he pleased. He could take her on the kitchen floor if he desired, and Natalie knew there wasn't a damn thing she could do about it. Would she even attempt to stop him, she wondered.

Much to her surprise, Nick stepped back, his face pinched, as though he were in a great deal of pain. "I've had too much to drink," he confessed without preamble. "I guess I'm not used to all this inactivity. I'm sorry if I, uh, did anything unbecoming a gentleman." There was laughter in his eyes as he gave a mock bow. "When I make love to you, I want to wake up the next morning and remember every detail." He sighed audibly while Natalie merely stared in bewilderment.

"But if this damn snow doesn't melt, I can't be held responsible for my actions," Nick added. "Especially if you wear that gown that shows off your nipples."

"I think it's time we ate," Natalie said quickly, opening the oven door and pulling out the pan of baked potatoes. She handed Nick his tray and tongs, and he walked to the fireplace to retrieve the steaks. Within five minutes Natalie had everything ready. She had placed the wine bottle out of sight and poured them each a cup of coffee. Nick returned with the steaks and put them on their plates.

The meal was eaten in silence, but Natalie watched Nick closely. When he drained his coffee cup, she dashed across the kitchen for the coffeepot and poured him another. He muttered his thanks without looking up.

Afterward Natalie suggested he take a shower while she cleaned the kitchen. He didn't argue; he seemed to think it a good idea.

By the time Nick emerged from the bathroom fresh and clean and wearing pajamas, Natalie had already cleaned the kitchen and laid out their bed just as Nick had done the night before. She saw the weary look on his face. "Tired?"

He nodded. "I need to build up the fire."

Natalie nodded and went into the bathroom to

brush her teeth and wash off her makeup. She knew Nick had probably used all the hot water, so a warm bath was out of the question. She dressed for bed, wearing her gown under Nick's robe.

She found Nick already asleep when she returned. A smile curled her lips as she turned off the remaining lights and sank down beside him. Automatically his body sought hers, and he pulled her spoon fashion against him.

Natalie wasn't shocked; in fact, she welcomed it.

The noise wouldn't go away. A low droning sound crept into Natalie's dreams. She opened her eyes and glanced around the room. Without rousing Nick, she slipped from the covers, tiptoed to the dining room at the front of the house, and peered out the window.

Snowplows! Two of them. Natalie raced back into the den and woke Nick. "They're here!"

"The North Vietnamese?" he asked, rising up as though ready to come out fighting. He'd been dreaming he and a couple of his buddies were in a foxhole waiting. When Nick figured out where he was, he gave Natalie a blank look. "Who's here?"

"The snowplows," she said excitedly. "They finally found your hideaway."

He frowned. "Is that why you woke me?" He buried his head in his pillow and went back to sleep.

Natalie didn't waste any time. She made coffee and searched for the telephone book. She found what she was looking for. "Is this Ned's Towing

Service?" she asked the gruff-sounding man who picked up at the other end of the line.

"That's what it says in the phone book, don't it?" he replied. "Wha'cha need towed in?"

"My car," Natalie said. "It's in a ditch about a mile from Nick Jordan's place. I ran off the road the night of the storm."

"And you been sleeping in your car ever since?" the man asked in disbelief.

"Well . . . uh . . . no," she answered. "Mr. Jordan was kind enough to let me spend a few nights at his place."

"Uh-huh."

"There really wasn't any other place to go."

"Yeah."

"Can you pull my car from the ditch or not?" she asked, irritated that she was trying to defend herself to some stranger.

"I can do it late this afternoon if the plows clear the road, but I got six cars ahead of yours."

Natalie sighed. "Okay, call me when you're ready." She gave him Nick's telephone number. Just as Natalie hung up, she was startled by a knock on the door. She opened it and found an attractive brunette wearing jeans and a ski jacket standing on the other side. The only flaw Natalie could find with the woman's appearance was the fact that she wore too much makeup. She was obviously surprised to find Natalie there.

"May I help you?" Natalie asked politely, worried there had been an accident. It was a bit early for visitors.

"I'd like to see Nick."

"I'm afraid he's asleep."

The woman shrugged. "Then wake him up. I didn't fight these roads for nothing."

"May I have your name?"

"Why, are you taking a census?" The woman smiled and walked through the doorway without waiting for an invitation. "Name's Irma. Nick will know who I am."

Six

Natalie froze at the words. Suddenly she smiled and clasped her hands together in delight. "You're *that* Irma," she said excitedly, remembering what Nick had said about the woman's temper. "I am *so* delighted to meet you," Natalie continued, taking the woman's hand and pumping it heartily. "Of course, I feel as if I already know you; Nick has told me so much."

The woman stared openly at Nick's robe. "He didn't mention you."

The moment Nick heard Irma's voice, he slid farther beneath the covers and buried his head beneath a pillow.

"Please let me take your coat," Natalie said, aware that Irma was gawking at the way she was dressed. Thank goodness she had covered her satin robe. "Come into the kitchen, and I'll pour you a cup of coffee."

The woman didn't miss seeing the bed in front of the fireplace or Nick's sleeping form outlined beneath the covers. "Is that Nick under there?"

Natalie set a cup of coffee on the table. "Oh, didn't he tell you? The furnace went out. We've closed off most of the house to keep warm, but we have to wear tons of clothes to keep from freezing to death," she added, emphasizing the word *tons*.

Nick decided it was time to face the music, so to speak, so he sat up and rubbed his eyes. "Irma! How good to see you. I take it the roads were clear enough for you to drive over."

She nodded. "I was right behind the plows. Would you mind telling me who this woman is who's wearing your robe?" she said without preamble and as though Natalie weren't in the room.

Nick and Natalie exchanged glances. Natalie was the first to speak. "Oh, I'm sorry, I assumed Nick told you I was here." She looked at Nick. "You didn't tell Irma I was staying here?"

"Uh, no . . . I haven't had a chance."

Natalie smiled at Irma. "I'm Natalie Courtland, Nick's sister from South Dakota." She held her breath. Nick had told her very little about his sister other than that she was married, lived in South Dakota, and had three children. But he had never mentioned whether Irma and his sister had met.

Irma seemed to warm up while Nick stared at Natalie with a look of incredulity. "Would you mind getting me a cup of coffee, sister dear?" he asked.

He took a seat at the table next to Irma and missed the dark look Natalie shot him. While he waited for Natalie to pour his coffee, Irma filled him in on the latest news. Natalie carried a mug of coffee over and set it before Nick, purposefully stepping on his toes as she did. The only indication that she had done so was the hardening of his jaw.

"Where is your family?" Irma asked Natalie. "I believe Nick told me you had children."

"Three," Natalie said, then glanced at Nick in the hope that she was right. He gave a slight nod that went unnoticed by Irma. Natalie pulled out a chair and took a seat between the two. "You want to know the truth, Irma?"

Nick almost choked on his coffee.

Irma nodded as though very interested.

"I left my husband. I got tired of playing nanny and maid when all he does is work. He never takes me out. Nick will tell you that. Tell her, Nick." She nudged him in what she thought was a sisterly fashion.

"He never takes her out," Nick said dully.

"So I told him he could take care of things for a while and that I was going on vacation. First thing he did was call his mother. Of course, I had no idea I was going to find myself right slap in the middle of a blizzard." She stood. "Well, I'd better take my shower. It was nice meeting you, Irma."

"Same here." Neither woman noticed the look of relief on Nick's face.

Natalie disappeared into the bathroom and lit the small heater. She paced back and forth, waiting for the room to warm up, wondering if Irma had swallowed her story.

"If that's your sister, I'll chew the tires off my jeep," Irma said once she and Nick were alone.

Nick didn't look up from his cup. "I knew you'd never fall for it. She got stranded in the snow, and I found her. She was suffering from hypothermia. She could have died." Nick suddenly wondered why he was going to such lengths to explain the situation to Irma. She had no claim on him nor he on her.

"When is she leaving?"

He shrugged. "Probably as soon as someone can pull her car out of a ditch. She hates this place."

"Where is she from?"

Nick raked his hand through his hair. "What is this, Twenty Questions?"

"I'm just concerned about your happiness. You of all people should know that." She reached over and patted his hand. "She's a pretty little thing. If her disposition comes anywhere close to her looks, you have a fine woman on your hands."

Her statement surprised him. "Forget it, Irma. She's a hotshot divorce lawyer from Atlanta. We haven't the slightest thing in common, and we don't get along worth a flip."

Irma smiled. "Sometimes those are the best relationships." She stood. "Well, I have to go." She patted him on the cheek.

"Wait, you left several books last time you were here. I've read them all. I'll go get them." Nick opened the door that led to the front of the house and shivered. He raced up the stairs to his bedroom in search of the paperbacks Irma had loaned him. Natalie stepped out of the bathroom wearing

Nick's robe, her hair twisted in a towel. She blushed, seeing Irma was still there. "Where's Nick?"

"He went upstairs to get some books I loaned him." They could hear Nick coming down the stairs. "I like you, Natalie," she said matter-of-factly. "Just don't hurt him."

Natalie didn't have a chance to respond. Nick came through the door with an armload of books. "I found a couple of others I had forgotten to return to you," he said.

"Nick and I both read horror novels," Irma told Natalie. "The scarier the better, right, Nick?" He nodded as he made his way to the door and opened it.

"Take care, Nick. And, Natalie, I hope you get your marital problems worked out." Irma had a funny smile on her face as Nick closed the door behind her.

Natalie wasn't sure what to make of Irma, but she understood one thing. The fact that Nick's eyes still remained in their sockets meant he had told the woman Natalie was going home soon—and they were probably making plans for themselves. Natalie gritted her teeth at the thought. So why had Irma warned Natalie not to hurt Nick? She sighed and shook her head. The world was certainly a complicated place.

It was well after five o'clock before Natalie's snow-crusted Jaguar was pulled out of the ditch. The layer of snow still left on the roads had already begun to freeze with the lowering temperature, so it had been tough getting the car out. Still, Natalie felt much better having her car parked outside Nick's house. Because of the snow, there had been no damage done when she had run into the ditch.

"It's too late to leave now," Nick said. "The roads are treacherous." He gave her a smile that curled her toes. "Besides, you won't have to share my bed tonight now that the furnace is working." Once Irma had left, Nick had immediately started making telephone calls. He'd paid an abominable sum in order to have the furnace repaired that day.

"I'm a big girl," Natalie said coolly, still convinced Nick and Irma had big plans for the evening. None of it made sense. Why wasn't Nick tossing her bags in the car if he had a hot night planned? And Irma's warning about not hurting Nick had played in Natalie's mind like a broken record all day. If the two of them were trying to throw her off by confusing her, they had succeeded. Natalie retrieved her belongings from the bathroom.

"Would you at least use common sense?" Nick shouted. "It's going to be like driving on glass. The snow itself was less dangerous. Wait until tomorrow afternoon. By then it should warm up and melt into slush."

Natalie relented if for no other reason than to put a damper on Nick and Irma's secret rendezvous, which she had thoroughly convinced herself of by the time she'd finished packing. Of course, that wouldn't prevent Nick from going to Irma's place. She was certain when Nick entered the den wearing new corduroy slacks and sweater that he was looking forward to a rewarding evening.

Natalie cursed herself for preparing a special meal of baked stuffed pork chops, a broccoli and cheese casserole, and corn on the cob. Nick couldn't believe his eyes. "How'd you find time to learn to cook and go to law school at the same time?"

Natalie refused to look at him, but she couldn't help smelling his tangy aftershave. "I learned to cook when I was very young. After my mother left. Are you going out?" she asked bluntly.

"And leave this delicious meal you've prepared?"

"Oh, so you're going to eat first, *then* go out."

"I have no intention of going out in this weather. Are you hoping to get rid of me?"

Natalie tried to hide her surprise. "No, I just thought—" She paused. "Never mind." She set the table, wondering why she felt so relieved Nick was staying home.

They talked comfortably over dinner, and Nick complimented her on the food so many times, Natalie blushed. Afterward she poured each of them a cup of coffee, and they settled on the sofa.

Nick looked amused. "I guess this is what married couples do."

Natalie shook her head. "Not the ones I work with. They yell and fight. They can't settle one dispute without going into combat. You'd be surprised how many marriages bite the dust every day."

"So, is that what turned you against it?"

Natalie nodded. "Handling divorce cases probably has had an effect on how I view marriage. Not to mention my own parents' divorce. It's not a pretty sight," she said grimly, and they both laughed.

"Incredible."

She shrugged. "What's incredible is the fact that some of the people liked each other enough to get married in the first place."

Nick set his coffee cup on the table in front of the couch. "No, I was talking about your complexion. It's perfect. There's not a blemish or flaw anywhere."

Natalie blushed. "That's because all the acne came and went the year I was in seventh grade."

"You're beautiful."

"Don't, Nick." Natalie edged away from him. "I'm leaving tomorrow. We've had a pleasant time together . . . most of the time. Let's not spoil our friendship."

"Friendship?" He laughed. "Lady, the last thing I want to be is your friend. I think lover is a better word."

"I'm leaving tomorrow," she repeated more firmly. "You shouldn't be saying these things to me."

"Am I to ignore the fact that I want you?"

The look on his face was so earnest. Natalie wondered how many nights she would fall asleep seeing that face in her mind. She would never forget the stolen kisses they'd shared.

He moved closer. "I always get what I want in the end."

His words angered her. She shot him a cold look. "How smug you are, Nick Jordan, to think I would just climb into your bed because you wished it. I think you're about to be disappointed." She started to get up from the couch, but Nick grabbed her by the wrist and halted her movement.

"Then what is it? There's got to be someone else."

"As I said before, that's none of your business."

"Has there *ever* been anyone?"

"My personal life is not your concern."

Suddenly he grabbed her by her arms and shook her hard. "It is when you think you're falling in love with that person, lady."

Natalie was stunned. Nick Jordan in love with her? After four days? She shook herself free. "That's the most ridiculous thing I've ever heard. You're mistaking lust for love."

Nick refused to let her go. "I could never have just plain sex with you, Natalie," he said, the timbre in his voice dropping seductively. "You were designed for lovemaking. Even the night I pulled you from the snow and had to undress you, I told myself I had never seen anything as exquisite as your body."

"And I thought you were trying to save my life," she muttered.

"I was trying to save your life, but I'm still a man. I wanted to press my lips against the birthmark on your inner thigh."

Natalie gasped in surprise. "You saw my birthmark?"

"I saw it all, lady," he said, taking delight in the rosy blush on her cheeks.

Natalie tried to twist free, but it was useless. "Nick Jordan, you're a sick man."

He laughed, grabbed her arm, and pulled her onto his lap despite her struggles. "No, I'm just a man smitten by a blue-eyed, blond-haired woman who tempts me beyond rational thought."

"I don't believe a word you're saying. I won't be gone five minutes when you'll go running back to Irma."

"You don't believe that."

"Let me up, Nick." When he released her, Natalie began to pace the floor. "This is the last time I'm going to tell you this, so listen good."

Nick's eyes were trained on her as she walked back and forth. "I'm listening." But his mind was elsewhere. Her designer jeans were snug and rode several inches above her trim ankles. The sweater she wore barely covered the waistband; every time she raised her arms he caught a glimpse of smooth flesh. What captivated him most, though, was the way her jeans hugged the sensual lines of her thighs and calves and molded perfectly to her round bottom.

"First of all, I've already told you how different our lives are. I studied very hard to become a lawyer, and it's taken me seven years of practice to prove myself in a courtroom. No, let me take that back. I've done *more* than prove myself. I've made a name for myself. My clients have lots of money, and I'm paid very well for my services. I live in a luxury condo, eat at the best restaurants and—"

"You've said enough, Natalie," he said in a dull voice. "You don't have to draw a picture for me. You're a very ambitious woman."

"Don't hate me for it, Nick. I suppose it's my way of building a secure life for myself. When you lose people you love, you feel the need to replace it with something else."

"I don't hate you. I feel sorry for you."

Natalie stood. "Pity is the last thing I'd expect to hear coming from your lips. You're still reliving the war. I've no doubt you've suffered, but you don't even try to put it behind you. That's why Irma is so convenient. She's nothing but a mere vessel where you empty your frustrations."

"That's enough, Natalie."

"Is it?" She planted her hands on her hips. The pain in his eyes tore at her heart. "Don't you think it's time you stopped blaming the human race for your problems? Maybe I have found other diversions to my loneliness, but I'm content with my life." She turned on her heel and headed toward the bedroom, slamming the door.

Natalie was too upset to think. Her mind was spinning wildly at the things Nick said. So, he thought her materialistic and ambitious, huh? If he had laughed at her car, he'd really get a kick out of her condo. True, she had surrounded herself with beautiful furnishings and clothes, but somehow seeing what she alone had accomplished made her feel better. It took some of the sting out of her memories. If she was strong enough to build such a successful life, surely she was strong enough to deal with the pain and disappointments life sometimes sent her way.

Damn! She had worked hard to build a successful life, and she was content—until Nick Jordan had begun to question her priorities. What did he know, stuck out here on a peach farm in the middle of nowhere? He may have saved her life, but he wasn't going to tell her how to live it.

She would be gone first thing in the morning. Five nights under the same roof with Nick Jordan were more than she could handle.

Seven

"Your Honor," Natalie said in a firm voice, "my client has not been allowed visitation with his children for six months, yet he continues to make generous monthly child support payments to his ex-wife. I have canceled checks to prove he has never been late on a payment. The divorce papers clearly state my client is to have his children every other weekend and one night during the week." Natalie stood at a long, narrow table beside her client, a man in his late thirties, not entirely oblivious to the hostile looks his ex-wife shot them both. You make a lot of enemies in this business, she thought.

Guy Pressman stood. "Your Honor, if I may approach the bench . . ."

The judge yawned. "I'd like counsel for the plaintiff *and* the defendant to approach the bench," he said sourly.

Natalie and Guy stepped forward. The judge didn't appear to be in the best of moods. Natalie could relate perfectly. Her disposition hadn't been the greatest over the past couple of weeks. *Ever since Nick Jordan had loaded her suitcases into her car and watched her drive away.*

Judge Morgan glared at the two attorneys. "What's going on here?" he demanded in a harsh whisper. "I've had this couple in my courtroom at least a half dozen times." He glared at Guy, then Natalie. "You're wasting my time and the taxpayers' dollars. Don't you two have any other cases?"

Natalie spoke first. "Your Honor, my client has lost all parental rights since the divorce. You yourself granted the couple joint custody due to the young ages of the children, but my client hasn't been able to spend any time with them. His wife has blatantly refused to abide by the court's orders."

"I love it when you get worked up over something, Natalie," Guy Pressman whispered. "Your eyes sparkle with fire."

Judge Morgan looked as though he'd like to use his gavel on the young attorney's head. Natalie glared at him. "Save it, Pressman," she muttered, knowing he did it half the time out of fun and the rest of the time to see how far he could push Judge Morgan, who just happened to be his uncle as well. "This is a courtroom, not a drive-in movie," she added.

Judge Morgan glanced at the clock at the back of the courtroom and sighed his relief. "Thank God it's five o'clock. I can't stand any more of this today." He slammed his gavel down several times loudly until he had the full attention of everyone present.

"Due to the lateness of the hour, this court will adjourn until nine o'clock Monday morning, at which time I'd like to see a little cooperation between the parties. Otherwise, I'm going to send an investigator into both homes to see if either of you is fit to raise children." He looked from the plaintiff to the defendant. "All this bickering back and forth can't be healthy for them. I may order them placed in a foster home until the two of you can work out your differences." Both clients paled instantly. The judge stood, stalked into his office, and slammed the door. A hush fell over the room before people started filing out.

"What in heaven's name is wrong with him today?" Guy asked Natalie.

"His gall bladder is probably acting up again." She hurried over to the table where her client sat and began stuffing papers in a folder. "Well, you heard him," she said. "Be back here at nine sharp on Monday."

"But, Miss Courtland—"

"Trust me, Mr. Davis. We'll get something worked out. That threat to send an investigator into both your homes is baloney. My instincts tell me Judge Morgan is merely trying to scare your wife. I'd be surprised if she didn't allow you to visit with your children this weekend." The man looked hopeful. "Just go home and try to relax." Natalie knew it would be an impossible task for the man as she watched him walk out of the courtroom with slumped shoulders.

"Want to join me for a drink?" Guy asked, coming up beside Natalie with his briefcase in hand.

She sat down if only to prevent being on eye level with Guy. "Not tonight. I'm going home, eating a frozen dinner, and hitting the sack. And by the way," she said, pressing her lips together in irritation, "no more wisecracks in front of the judge. How about practicing a little professionalism in the courtroom, Pressman?"

"Heartless wench," he muttered good-naturedly. "One of these days I'm going to stop asking you out."

"My loss," she quipped, closing her briefcase and snapping the locks. She took off her reading glasses and put them into a pouch in her purse. "See you Monday," she told Guy as he made his way out of the courtroom, taking a minute to speak to the red-headed court stenographer.

Natalie sat there for a while. The silence of the empty courtroom was a pleasant relief after a hectic day. Sometimes she spent the entire day at the courthouse with files stacked in her briefcase, running from courtroom to courtroom in order to make her appearances on time. She rolled her head back and forth, stretching her sore neck muscles, trying to work out the tension. She had been uptight all week, and having to deal with the Davises was a chore she didn't relish.

Natalie wondered about her tiredness. Could it be that she was just depressed and didn't know it? Not hearing from Nick had made her sink a bit lower each day. Her father believed her to be anemic. She sighed heavily and stood, then grabbed her briefcase and slipped through the waist-high swinging door that separated the lawyers and clients from the onlookers. The rat-tat-tat of her high heels sounded strange in the deathly quiet of the courtroom.

So what if Guy thought her a party pooper, she told herself. True, she had no social life to speak of, but it was probably just as well given her work load. At least she didn't fuddle through half her cases as though she hadn't even bothered to look them over as he sometimes did after a busy weekend. She had been working late every night, if not at the office then at home. Even to herself she wouldn't admit she was trying to keep her mind off Nick Jordan. Inside, though, she knew it for a fact. She had not been able to get him off her mind no matter how hard she'd tried.

Natalie made her way down the aisle, and from the corner of her eye caught movement in the back row. She glanced up quickly.

Nick Jordan looked very much at home sitting there munching on popcorn.

Natalie came to a screeching halt as she stared in disbelief. She blinked several times, wanting to make sure it was he. But then, she couldn't mistake those compelling brown eyes and that handsome face any more than she could her own. It had become permanently fixed in her mind.

"Nick!" She paused, not knowing exactly what to say. He shot her a grin that told her he was enjoying her stupefied reaction. "What are you doing here?" Natalie finally asked.

"I need a lawyer."

She laughed nervously. "I'm afraid you've come to the wrong place. Cowpens, South Carolina, is a bit out of the area in which I practice."

"Maybe I should have put it another way," he said, unfolding himself from the seat. "I wasn't trying to solicit your . . . uh . . . professional skills." His eyes roamed over her body freely. "Want some popcorn?"

She shook her head dumbly. Natalie hadn't forgotten how tall he was, how broad his shoulders. His corduroy jacket strained against hard muscles, and his jeans were tight, molding nicely to his thighs. She swallowed. "How's your peach crop?" she said, trying to get her thoughts off his body.

"Believe it or not, I think much of it's going to survive. Of course, it won't be one of my best years . . . where peaches are concerned," he added. His peach crop had become second to his thoughts of Natalie. He still remembered the day he'd loaded her luggage into her car and had watched her drive away, a sinking feeling in his gut. He hadn't removed the sheet on the bed where she'd slept, and he had an odd habit of going into the room and burying his face against her pillow and inhaling her scent.

Natalie was still trying to maintain her composure when all she wanted to do was throw herself into Nick's arms. "So what brings you to Atlanta?" She spoke flippantly, as though seeing him again were of little consequence. The last thing she wanted him to guess was how deliriously happy she was or how desperately she had missed him. For all she knew, he and Irma had picked up where they'd left off before the storm. She thought about them every night as she lay in bed, so much in fact, she suffered terrible bouts of insomnia. She hoped the dark circles beneath her eyes didn't show.

He shrugged. "I've got some business with my brother."

"The investor?" She tried to keep the disappointment out of her voice. So he had not come specifically to see her. Her heart sank. Still, he looked and smelled wonderful. His hair had been fashionably cut and styled, unlike the longer, mussed look she'd grown accustomed to that made him look as though he'd just climbed out of some woman's bed.

Nick nodded. "Yeah, every time I make a dime he wants me to invest in something. Last time it was tuna fish." They both laughed. But Nick felt the strain between them and wondered if he'd been right to come. "Remember when I said I'd like to see you in action in the courtroom?"

"Yes, although I can't imagine why."

"I wanted to see what you were like. I called your office, and the receptionist told me you were going to be in court all afternoon, so here I am. It has been hell trying to follow you from courtroom to courtroom without your seeing me."

Natalie laughed. "I can't believe you wasted an

afternoon sitting in courtrooms listening to petty arguments between couples."

"I was watching you."

The spell of his voice and the way his gaze captured hers briefly before dropping to her lips made breathing difficult for Natalie. "Oh?"

"I wanted to see what you wore, how you handled yourself. I was right about one thing."

"Oh?"

"You're a tigress in the courtroom as well." He lowered his voice to a whisper. "If you're half as feisty in bed, you're going to make one helluva lover."

"Nick—" She glanced around nervously, thankful no one was around.

"You're a fine lawyer, Natalie Courtland. After watching you operate, I can't imagine you being in any other profession." He laughed. "For some reason I couldn't picture you in a courtroom when you were wearing my robe. Now, with that snazzy three-hundred-dollar suit and those glasses, you look like the real thing." He was surprised some enterprising male client hadn't set her up in style. Perhaps it was that aloof, strictly-business attitude she emanated that kept them from trying.

She smiled. For some reason Nick's opinion mattered very much. "Can I buy you a cup of coffee or a cold beer?" she asked.

He grinned. "I was holding my breath hoping you'd ask."

He gave her the same smile that sent her pulse racing. Being around Nick did things to her insides that would have sent most folks running to the doctor. She had forgotten how her stomach dipped every time he smiled at her or how her heart pounded in her ears when he was near. So why hadn't he called her? She had checked her answering machine over and over, hoping to hear Nick's voice.

"There's a little place across the street," she heard herself saying. "Nothing fancy."

"Good. I don't like fancy."

Nick took her briefcase and motioned her ahead. "After you, Counselor." He tossed his empty popcorn box into a trash can outside the courtroom.

Ten minutes later they were seated at a small table in a crowded bar and grill. Natalie wiped her damp palms on her skirt beneath the table. Her heart hadn't stopped racing since she'd spotted Nick sitting in the back row of the courtroom. Suddenly it all came rushing back—the kisses, the heat from his hard body as he'd held her through the night when the furnace had quit.

"What are you thinking?"

Natalie looked up, startled. "Nothing really. I guess I'm just so surprised you're here, that's all."

"Did I make a mistake by coming?"

"No, of course not." When the waitress finally came to their table, Natalie didn't order wine as she usually did. Instead she ordered something stronger, hoping it would make her relax. She felt as skittish as a coon with a pack of hounds on his scent.

"So, is this where all the lawyers hang out?" Nick asked when the waitress had left them. He looked around at the men dressed in three-piece suits and was certain this was where her colleagues came to unwind. No doubt he resembled Amos McCoy with his jeans and worn corduroy jacket. He *had* made a mistake in coming after all. But damn, he'd wanted to see her. If he thought for one moment he was embarrassing her . . .

She nodded. "It's cheap and close to the courthouse. And the food is pretty good." She sensed his discomfort immediately and tried to start a conversation. "Who's watching Daisy and the puppies?"

"A friend," he said vaguely. "You should see the size of those pups."

Natalie wondered if Irma was the friend but didn't ask. The waitress arrived with their drinks, and Natalie felt like hugging the woman for the distraction. Natalie took a long gulp of her drink, then she suddenly realized Nick was speaking to her.

". . . And I was wondering if you'd like to join us for dinner."

Her head snapped up. "I'm sorry, I didn't catch everything you said."

Nick gave her a funny look. "Are you okay, Natalie? You look as if you're about to jump out of your skin." What a stupid question, he thought. She'd probably dated half the guys in the place and now here she was with some backwoods hillbilly.

Was it that obvious, she wondered. She had missed him so much that it took every ounce of self-discipline to keep from taking his big hand in hers or stroking his cheek. But he hadn't made a move, and she had no idea where she stood with him. "I've just had a long week. It usually takes me a couple of hours to unwind."

"I know the perfect remedy for that," he said, giving her a devilish grin.

"So you've told me. Did I hear you invite me to dinner?"

"Yes. My brother Arthur will be there. Hope you don't mind."

"Of course not," she said, a little disappointed. She had hoped to spend the evening alone with Nick.

They talked for a while longer, Natalie drinking in the sight of him. After the past two weeks without having heard a word from him, she'd been certain he was out of her life forever.

"Earth to Natalie. Come in, please."

Natalie blinked. "Did you say something?" Her befuddled brain wouldn't cooperate, for some reason.

"I asked you to give me your address. This isn't Cowpens. I can't just drive up and down the streets till I find your car."

Natalie rattled off the address and watched him write it on a cocktail napkin in large bold strokes. His hands—Lord, she'd never forget the size of those hands or how they'd felt on her skin. Her stomach fluttered at the memory.

Nick looked up and caught her staring. He saw the funny little smile on her face. "Anything wrong?"

"Oh, I was just thinking." Her gaze met his and locked, and she knew he was thinking about their time together as well. Despite all the discomforts, the five days and nights they'd shared had been the most wonderful time of her life. Suddenly she laughed. "I was remembering the morning I got locked in the shower with ice water spraying on me."

Nick smiled at the thought, but he preferred to remember the moment he swooped her from the tub and kissed her. She had tasted sweeter than nectar. One breast had peeked out from the towel, and he'd wanted to cup it in his hands, suck it, flick the coral nipple with his tongue until it was tight. Yes, he remembered. What man in his right mind could forget?

Nick's thoughts seemed far away at the moment, and Natalie knew he was remembering the kiss. She could see it in the way his eyes darkened. They had shared several kisses—delicious, titillating kisses that had spread warmth through her lower belly like good brandy.

"I—I think I'd better go now," Natalie said hesitantly, fearing Nick could read the emotions on her face. Perhaps it was best that his brother was joining them. "Would you like me to meet you and your brother at the restaurant?"

"And miss the opportunity of riding in the Blue Goose?"

She shook her head slightly and laughed. "The what?"

"My old blue pickup truck."

"Oh." She laughed. "Will Arthur be riding with us?"

"Are you kidding? He'd die first. He's a Mercedes

man." Nick laughed. "I love parking in front of his swank garden apartment and blowing the horn. It brings out all the neighbors. They usually stare at me and my truck as though the Beverly hillbillies had just come to town." They both laughed out loud. "Arthur won't even come out. He stands in the doorway and motions for me to come inside. Of course, he always finds another place for me to park, like near the garbage dumpster."

"Don't tell me he's a snob."

Nick shrugged. "Okay, I'll just let you find out for yourself."

Natalie laughed so hard, she had tears in her eyes. "He sounds like my father. Perhaps we should introduce them. Does he golf?"

"Every chance he gets. He plays at the Atlanta Athletic Club." He saw her nod. "Your father too? Actually Arthur doesn't care much for the game, but he says it's a good way to meet potential investors."

Natalie studied him, feeling more comfortable. "So how come you didn't turn out to be a snob?"

Nick's gaze was fastened to her lips as she spoke. In his mind he could still remember how soft they were, how they meshed so easily with his own. He would love to guide her lips all over his body. He tried to concentrate on their conversation. "My parents were very humble farmers, not the least bit snobbish. My sister is the same. Money and clothes don't impress her. I suppose when you know you can't have it, you don't expect it. Arthur was always different. My father mortgaged the farm to put him through college."

"Why did your sister move away?"

"She married, and her husband was transferred. Besides, neither she nor Arthur cared anything about the farm. In fact, Arthur wanted to sell it and divide the money. So I bought them out. Eventually," he added.

Natalie nodded, then glanced at her wristwatch. "Look at the time. I really need to go home and shower."

He grinned. "Would you like my help? As I recall, you have a problem where showers are concerned."

She gave him a haughty look. "Well, for your information, my shower doesn't dump ice water on my head."

"Neither would mine if you hadn't dawdled."

"I have never . . . dawdled in my life." She felt herself blush. How could the man turn a simple word into something sensual? It automatically brought a picture to her mind of them showering together. Nick's chest would be wide and powerful and matted with hair. His stomach would be flat and hard, his navel surrounded by dark brown hair that curled around his sex . . . *Stop it!* she told herself.

Natalie stood up so fast, she sent her chair toppling to the floor, but Nick caught it in time. "I have to go."

He nodded. "Yes, I see that. When you're ready to go, you don't mess around." He picked up the cocktail napkin with her address on it.

"Do you think you can find it?"

"I'll find it."

Nick paid at the register, and walked her to her

car. He waited until she had unlocked it and gotten in. She rolled down her window. "What time should I be ready?"

"Is eight o'clock okay?" She nodded. "Lock your doors and roll up your windows."

Natalie pressed her lips together. "I'm a big girl, Nick."

He grinned, and somehow it made him look younger; the lines around his mouth weren't as harsh. "I think that's what I like best about you."

Eight

Natalie felt as though she were floating on a cloud as she checked her reflection in the mirror. She wore a black crepe dress that was tapered at the hem and a wide belt that emphasized her trim waist. Her jewelry consisted of a single strand of pearls. She checked her apartment. It was a decorator's dream. The forest green and plum flame-stitch-patterned sofa, the two stark white tulip chairs, and the lacquered tables created an elegant setting that could have graced the cover of a magazine. Her collection of antique music boxes was displayed throughout the room.

A bottle of white wine sat chilling in a bucket. She frowned. Nick would probably prefer beer. She should have thought of that.

When the doorbell pealed a few minutes before eight, Natalie jumped, then placed her right hand over her heart as though to keep it from leaping out of her chest. Taking a deep breath and patting her short blond hair in place, she checked the peephole and saw Nick's handsome face.

Natalie opened the door but was in no way prepared for the sight of the man on the other side. Gone were the jeans, flannel shirt, and corduroy jacket. Instead, Nick wore brown pleated slacks, a blue shirt with thin brown stripes, and a brown herringbone sport coat. They stared at each other for a full minute before Natalie thought to invite him in.

"You look nice," she said.

"You look beautiful; but then, you always do."

The minute Nick stepped over the threshold, he handed Natalie a box. She looked up in surprise. "Candy? How thoughtful." And romantic. She smiled. "Are you trying to make me fat?"

"It's okay," he said, giving her a slip of a grin. "I ate half the box on the way over. First meal I've had today except for the popcorn."

Natalie laughed. "Then I'm not sure if I should offer you a glass of wine."

"Go ahead, I'm a big boy."

This time Natalie grinned, thankful he hadn't requested a beer instead. "So I've noticed." She picked up a corkscrew and handed it to him.

Arthur Jordan was undoubtedly one of the most boring and conceited men Natalie had ever met. His double chin and soft stomach told her he indulged too much in liquor, but then, if she had to spend much time with him, she would probably turn to alcohol, too, she thought. She supposed he was in his mid-forties and he supposed he was an expert on any subject. No wonder he was divorced, she thought. He didn't need a wife, he needed a full-time audience.

"You didn't really drive up in the Blue Goose?" Arthur asked his brother as though it would cause a scandal he would never live down. "This is Anthony's of Atlanta, not some greasy spoon in Cowpens."

Nick and Natalie exchanged smiles. "Actually it was very funny," she said. "Nick told the valet he was driving a relic that was going to be on display at the next World's Fair. I think the poor kid was scared to drive it after that." She glanced around at her surroundings. Anthony's had at one time been a large antebellum home. Now it consisted of several small dining rooms.

"Why don't you buy something decent to drive, Nick?" Arthur said, sipping his third martini. "It's not as if you can't afford it."

"Affording and wanting are two separate things," Nick said simply. He glanced around. "Could you point me in the direction of the men's room?" Arthur motioned toward the back of the restaurant, and Nick excused himself, giving Natalie a heart-wrenching smile. "Would you excuse me? I'll be right back." She smiled and nodded.

Arthur polished off his drink and ordered another. "So, Natalie, you're a divorce lawyer."

She smiled serenely. "That's right."

"I remember reading an article about you when they did a write-up on some of the top executive women in Atlanta. I understand you can get down-right nasty in court."

"If I have to. But then, most divorce cases end up getting nasty."

"I wish you'd been around when I needed a good lawyer. My wife got everything except the clothes off my back. She has convinced the kids to go to Harvard when they graduate high school. I think she did it just to give me ulcers. I buy Maalox by the case." He put his hand on Natalie's knee. "Some women are nothing but bloodsuck-ers. Know what I mean?"

She gave him another sweet smile. "I've been fortunate not to meet many. Arthur, do you know what Mace is?"

He shrugged, obviously confused by the quick turn of conversation. "Some chemical that burns like hell if it's sprayed in a person's face," he said in a disinterested voice.

Natalie nodded. "That's right. And if you don't release my knee, I'm going to spray it right be-tween your eyes."

He let go instantly. "Sorry, Natalie. I was just trying to be friendly." His drink was delivered, and he took a sip. "I see you go for country boys like ol' Nick." He shrugged. "He plays a good game, I'll give him that."

"What are you talking about?" Natalie wondered if Arthur even knew what *he* was talking about. He had definitely had too much to drink.

"Nick's loaded. And if I may be so humble, I've made some pretty good investments for him. He probably owns half the land in Cowpens now, not to mention the cannery."

"What cannery?" she asked dully, wishing Nick would hurry.

"*The* cannery. It's the largest in the Southeast. Employs half the town of Cowpens. He cans the finest peaches in the south," Arthur said, holding his martini glass in midair. He put it to his lips and drained it.

Nick returned to the table and gave Natalie an apologetic smile. "Sorry, there was a line."

The waiter brought their menus to the table and passed them out. "Could you bring me another drink?" Arthur held up his empty glass.

"Don't you think you've had enough?" Nick asked, sporting a frown.

Arthur ignored him and ordered the drink anyway. "Nick hasn't always been this way, Natalie," Arthur said, slurring his words. "We raised hell when we were kids." He glanced at Nick. "Did we raise hell or not?"

Nick nodded, giving him a placating smile. "Yeah, we did."

"Then ol' Nick got shipped off to Vietnam while I was in college, and that was that. Straight out of high school too. He wasn't there six months before he fell for some little Vietnamese gal—hell, I never could remember her name."

"I'm sure Natalie isn't interested," Nick said, shifting in his chair uncomfortably.

Arthur slapped Nick on the back. "Fathered a son, too, didn't you?"

Natalie sat frozen to her chair. She didn't know what to do or say. Nick's face looked as though it were made of marble. She was thankful when the salads arrived.

Dinner was a long-drawn-out affair. Arthur, who claimed he ate at Anthony's every week, insisted on ordering for them. Natalie's head ached miserably, and she wanted to go home. Nick hadn't so much as glanced in her direction since Arthur had mentioned his past.

"Don't you like the food, Natalie?" Arthur asked.

She forced a smile. "I'm afraid I'm not very hungry."

Arthur frowned at Nick. "And here I was trying to impress your lady friend by inviting ya'll to the nicest place in town. Hell, if I had known she wasn't hungry, we could have gone for hamburgers." He laughed, and the sound reverberated around the room, causing several people to stare.

"Arthur, don't order another drink," Nick said sternly.

The rest of the meal was strained. Natalie had never been so uncomfortable in her life. First there was Arthur, who was doing his best to make a fool of himself. Then there was the discovery that Nick had at one time fathered a child and was a wealthy man. He certainly didn't play the part. Why had he kept it from her? Her mind whirled with a dozen questions.

Once their dinner plates were removed, Natalie

and Nick ordered coffee, and Arthur ordered a flaming Irish whiskey. "Dessert anyone?" he asked, his mood festive.

"No thank you," Natalie replied. "I'd really like to go home now," she implored Nick. "This has been a very long day for me." Not to mention the evening, she thought.

When the check was presented to Arthur, Nick snatched it from his hand. Arthur looked surprised. "Save your money for cab fare," Nick said as he handed the waiter a credit card with the check. "Would you mind calling a taxi for my brother?" The waiter nodded and left them.

Once the waiter returned with Nick's card, he signed the receipt and stood. Arthur sat in a half stupor. "Look after him and see that he takes the taxi." He searched for a piece of paper and scribbled on it. "Here's the address in case he passes out. Oh, one more thing—" Nick reached into his pocket. "Here's cab fare and a generous tip. Tell the driver to help him into the apartment if necessary."

The waiter nodded. "It will be done as you wish, sir."

Natalie and Nick waited for his truck to be brought around. Nick was relieved to see the taxi had already arrived. Once he helped Natalie in and slammed the door, he tipped the valet and climbed in on his side. He drove awhile in silence. "I'm sorry the evening turned out as it did," he finally said. "I had no idea Arthur was hitting the bottle like that. I mean, he always drank, but not to that extent."

"I was just happy to spend the evening with you, Nick," Natalie said simply.

He glanced at her in surprise. He'd been certain after the scene Arthur made, Natalie would never want to see him again.

Once they arrived at Natalie's condo, she invited Nick up for coffee. The doorman tipped his hat at Natalie as she passed with Nick in tow, and both of them stood patiently at the elevators.

When they reached Natalie's apartment, she went about making a pot of coffee, while Nick studied his surroundings. He opened the sliding glass door that led to the balcony and walked out to gaze at the city lights. He and Natalie were worlds apart, he thought. He had suspected as much in the beginning, but seeing her in her own environment merely confirmed the fact.

That didn't stop him from wanting her.

"Oh, there you are." Natalie joined Nick on the balcony. "Isn't it beautiful?" she asked, indicating the horizon of lights. "Sometimes when I can't sleep or I can't get my mind off a case, I sit out here."

He shrugged. "I guess it depends on your preference."

"How so?"

"Some people prefer star-gazing while others enjoy city lights."

"And which do you prefer?"

Even in the dark his smile was easily visible. "I think you know the answer to that."

Natalie felt a dull ache in her stomach. They stared at the scene before them in comfortable silence for a while, then Natalie slipped away to pour their coffee. She returned and handed a cup to Nick. Although there was a small table and chairs situated in the corner of the balcony, they stood at the railing, sipping their coffee.

"This is a nice change from the solitude of country life, though," Nick said, trying to make up for his previous statement. He had probably hurt her feelings, and that was the last thing he'd wanted to do.

Natalie didn't really believe him. "What happened in Vietnam, Nick?" she blurted out without warning after having bitten back the question a hundred times.

He looked mildly surprised. "There was a war between the North Vietnamese and the South. We were trying to prevent a Communist takeover." He said it without emotion, as though he'd tried to explain it many times, perhaps to himself, and now it sounded like a recording.

"I know what the war was about," Natalie said. "I want to know about Nick Jordan's war. Something happened to you over there, didn't it?"

He gave her a snort of a laugh. "You mean besides seeing the killing and maiming?" She didn't answer. He knew she was waiting for the truth, and knowing the attorney side of Natalie, she wouldn't give up until she got it.

Nick gazed down at his big hands. "I was just a kid then." He looked at Natalie speculatively. "Have you ever wondered why they send eighteen-year-old kids out to fight wars?" When she didn't respond right away, he went on. "When you're eighteen, you're so damn stupid you don't know the odds of getting your head blown off." He laughed at that, but it wasn't a happy sound. "Try recruiting a bunch of thirty-year-old men, and they'll tell you to go to hell. They're not going to sit in a foxhole for hours or chop their way through tall grass in search of the enemy, when they haven't the slightest idea who the enemy is. Hell no, let some pimple-faced kid do the job."

Nick set his coffee cup down on the table behind him and clutched the railing tightly as he stared at the view without really seeing it. He felt Natalie's hand on his shoulder, and surprisingly enough the frustration and anger boiling in his gut gentled. He turned and caught her around the waist. "You'r beautiful," he whispered, taking her coffee cup and placing it beside his own. "Beautiful and sweet and untouched by bitterness."

She gave a nervous laugh. "I have my ghosts, Nick. But why are you so bitter? Why have you chosen to separate yourself from the rest of the world?"

"It was a long time ago, Natalie."

"But you're still suffering. Why?"

He didn't answer right away. When he turned away from her and grasped the railing once more, she was afraid he wasn't going to answer. "My story is no different from a lot of others, I'm sure," he said. "I fell in love with a South Vietnamese girl."

"Me Lin?" she whispered.

He nodded. "We had a son, a big robust boy

that would make any father proud." He shook his head. "As if I knew anything about being a father. Like I said, I was just a kid. The day U.S. troops were told they were going home was one of the happiest days of my life. Me Lin and I began planning how to get her and the baby to the States. I flew home with stars in my eyes. We were going to be married in the little church in Cowpens." He stopped talking.

"What happened?" Natalie prodded gently.

When Nick spoke, his voice was devoid of expression. "Me Lin's village was attacked just after the fall of Saigon. Me Lin and the baby were murdered."

Natalie's stomach lurched forward at the confession. For a moment all she could do was stare at the tall silhouette of the man beside her. Then, suddenly, she felt tears streaming down her cheeks. She was crying for the man whose pain had lasted so many years and the injustices brought on by war. "I'm so sorry, Nick," she said, as though personally responsible for it all.

"I promised Me Lin I would get her and the baby out. I promised. She trusted me. I let her down."

"Nick, you certainly couldn't help what happened back there."

"And then I deceived her."

"How, for heaven's sake?"

He turned his head in her direction although he maintained a tight grip on the railing. "By falling in love with you," he ground out.

If Natalie had been shocked before, it was nothing compared to the way Nick's confession of love affected her. "I don't know what to say," she finally admitted.

He turned to her. "You could say the feeling was mutual."

She could. She wanted to. But where would that leave them? "Nick—"

"Don't say it unless you mean it, Natalie. I don't want pretty lies coming from your lips."

She hung her head as a fresh batch of tears filled her eyes. "You don't understand," she said with a gulp.

He put a finger beneath her chin and raised her gaze to his. "I think I do, Counselor. You've surrounded yourself with beautiful things. This condo, the clothes you wear, the car you drive. What else could you possibly need? You're a bit like Arthur, I think." Although he didn't believe it for a moment, he wanted to wound her as she had wounded him by not reciprocating his feelings.

Natalie's hand itched to slap his face at the barb. "Then you really don't know me at all," she said tightly.

"I know I'd rather stand than sit on your furniture. It looks as if it belongs on a showroom floor, not in someone's home. I know that I want to kiss you, but I'm scared I'll muss that perfect hair or that china-doll makeup on your face." He reached for his coffee cup, drained it, and set it down. "I think it's time I left," he said, already stepping through the sliding glass doors.

"That's not fair!" Natalie shouted, clutching her

fists by her sides. Her eyes burned with tears of pain and anger. "Listen to me, Nick," she said as he made his way toward the door. "Maybe I have surrounded myself with beautiful things. But I work hard. I deserve them. I deserve to dress in designer clothes, eat at the best restaurants. It's all I have, Nick, don't you understand?" She couldn't tell whether he was listening. "Of course I surround myself with pretty things." A sob ripped from her throat. "I've lost everybody I ever loved. At least these things can be replaced."

All at once Natalie felt him take her in his arms as her tears racked her slender frame. She felt his lips on her hair, his voice soothing her. She clung to him as though her very life depended on it. Nick's lips caught each tear, and when his mouth found hers, the kiss was gentle.

"Don't hate me for the way I am, Nick," she said against his lips.

"I don't hate you. I love you. You're beautiful. And I'm going to mess up your hair." This time his mouth was hot and demanding. His tongue speared its way past her lips, and he moaned as he tasted the sweetness inside.

"To hell with my hair," she managed to say. "Just don't stop kissing me or holding me." Natalie went weak with pleasure. Nick's mouth was everywhere. His hands slipped through her hair and tilted her head so that there was not a place untouched by his lips. She could feel the fires stoking in her belly, spreading heat through her thighs. Nick pressed himself against her, and desire shot through her body as she felt his blatant need. He reached for her belt, and it fell to the carpeted floor with a whisper. Her hands unfastened the buttons on his shirt as he reached around and worked down the zipper on her dress. Nick pulled the dress off her shoulders, kissing each lovely slope he bared. He shrugged off his jacket and tossed it aside.

When the dress slid to the floor next to his jacket, Nick gazed at Natalie with unveiled desire. Her black bra and half slip worked like an aphrodisiac on his senses. He removed the slip, stared in disbelief at the black garter belt. "It must be my birthday."

Natalie smiled coyly. "Do you like the wrappings?"

"Lady, I'm about to show you just how much." He swooped her up high in his arms and carried her toward a door, his lips fastened to hers.

"Closet," she said against his mouth, then motioned in the direction of her bedroom.

Nick felt himself straining against the fabric of his slacks and mentally ordered himself to slow down. As he walked through the door leading to her bedroom, he caught a brief glimpse of a white eyelet bedspread and curtains. Heart-shaped and oval pillows trimmed with lace and ribbons cluttered the bed, and as he lay Natalie down, he swept them onto the floor.

Once again his lips captured hers in a deep, soul-searching kiss. His eager hands worked at the clasp of her bra, and he cursed the manufacturers of female lingerie. Natalie laughed, reached around, and easily unhooked it. The bra fell forward, and Nick sucked in his breath at the sight of her perfect white breasts. He cupped them in his palms and flicked the coral nipples lightly before taking one between his lips.

Natalie raked her hands through his hair and held him close. Her heart swelled with love for the man. His touch, his kiss, even his scent seemed as if they had been created just for her. Nick shrugged out of his shirt impatiently. Natalie delighted in the crisp curls that covered his wide chest and slid her fingers through them as she had longed to do since she had first seen him wearing only his pajama bottoms that morning at his house.

Nick tongued her nipples until they stood erect and quivering, then moved his lips down her abdomen. He reached for one of the hooks on her garter belt and worked it free. His eyes were dark with desire. "Remind me to order you a dozen more just like this," he said, kissing each spot he bared. Her stockings were unlike anything he'd ever felt—pure silk and sexy as hell. Once she was wearing nothing but a pair of lacy black panties, he sighed heavily. "I would have never made it through dinner if I'd known you were wearing these."

Natalie smiled, pleased that he found her desirable. She closed her eyes as his lips brushed her inner thigh. All at once she felt his mouth hot and raspy against the panties, and a moan of sheer pleasure escaped her lips.

Nick almost tore the wispy black lace from her body. When Natalie lay before him completely naked, he could only stare. The triangle of dark gold curls tempted him beyond rational thought.

Nick's tongue teased and tormented her until Natalie thought she would lose her mind. His hands stroked her sensitive inner thigh. She cried out as a feeling of sheer delight washed over her body. Nevertheless, Nick continued creating his magic, even after the waves of passion had subsided. Before long Natalie was once again caught up in intense pleasure.

She reached for his belt, but Nick stood and began unfastening it with deliberate slowness as he gazed into her hungry, passion-filled eyes. When he was completely naked, he joined her.

The mattress dipped beneath his weight. Natalie automatically went to him. She kissed his chest, his wide shoulders, his neck, and then hesitantly reached for his swollen sex. He moaned aloud at her touch.

"I love you, Nick." The words left her lips of their own volition.

A flicker of emotion passed over his face as he swept her thighs apart and entered her, filling her with himself. He closed his eyes against the agony of pleasure. Nick kissed her, his tongue sending flames through her body. His hands caressed her breasts as he thrust evenly into her, cursing the satin folds that grasped him so tightly. Natalie cried out as she reached the height of pleasure. She heard Nick's gasp as he shuddered against her and filled her with a delicious warmth.

After several minutes their erratic heartbeats slowed and their breathing became normal. Nick raised himself up from Natalie, moved beside her, and gathered her in his arms. "I could grow accustomed to this, lady."

Natalie smiled sleepily. "So could I."

"Thank you." He kissed her tenderly.

She looked surprised. "For what?"

"For teaching me that making love can be terrific at any age."

She frowned. "You're not *that* old, for heaven's sake."

"Old enough to know when I've found the real thing."

Nine

Natalie glared at Nick over the rim of her coffee cup the next morning. She was propped on several pillows on her bed. "I hope you're as tired as I am," she said.

He grinned. "Not at all. In fact, I couldn't go to sleep last night."

"So I noticed. I need to sit in a hot tub for an hour."

A look of concern crossed his face. "Did I hurt you?"

She reached up and stroked his cheek, realizing she loved him more with each passing minute. "I'm okay. It's just—"

"What?"

"Never mind."

He frowned. "I hate it when people do that to me."

She glanced away from him. "It has been a long time."

Male ego alone made him ask. "How long?"

Natalie's face burned. "Nick!"

"Tell me."

She sighed heavily. "Since college."

"Were you in love with him?"

"I thought I was. I think it was infatuation."

"What about us?" he asked, a frown creasing his forehead. "How do you know this isn't infatuation?"

She smiled coyly. "Because I would have to be deeply in love with a man to do all those naughty things you taught me last night."

"Guess what?"

"Hmm?"

He took her coffee cup and set it aside. "We only skimmed the surface." He jerked the sheet off her, and she shrieked. "Don't go modest on me now, Counselor. I've already seen every delectable inch of your body."

"You have no scruples, Nick Jordan."

He pulled her body tight against him. "That's right. And neither will you when I'm finished." His mouth came down on hers, and the growth of a night's beard felt wonderful and sexy against Natalie's cheek.

He entered her slowly and found her wet. "Sore?"

Natalie wrapped her arms around his neck and met the thrust evenly. She gave him a saucy smile. "Not anymore." Nick made love to her very gently. Afterward she curled up in his arms and drifted off to sleep.

• • •

When Natalie opened her eyes she noticed it was past noon. She glanced at the spot beside her and found it empty. Anxiously she sat up, holding the sheet to her breasts. "Nick?" she called out.

He stepped out of the bathroom wearing a towel around his waist. "So you finally decided to wake up, eh?" He saw the look on her face. "What's wrong?"

"Oh, nothing," she lied. "I just didn't mean to sleep so late." She wasn't about to confess that she'd been afraid he'd left.

"I'm starving," he said. "There is nothing edible in your refrigerator."

"That's not true. There's yogurt, skim milk, and bran cereal."

"Like I said, nothing edible. Now, get your pert little fanny in the shower and dressed before I starve."

"Would you hand me my robe? It's lying across that chair."

He grinned and crossed his arms over his wide chest. "Nope."

"Nick!"

"Okay, just this once." He tossed it to her. "You've got twenty minutes to get ready. And stop locking the bathroom door. If I want in, there's not a lock in this world that's going to stop me."

"What about my privacy?"

"You lost it last night."

She pursed her lips. "You're indecent."

"Thank you. You now have eighteen minutes left. If you need my help—"

"That won't be necessary." She was already scrambling into the robe.

"I highly recommend this place," Natalie said, leading Nick into a modern restaurant filled with hanging plants. They were ushered to a table and handed menus.

Nick scanned the listings. "Do they serve steak?"

"No, but they have quiche, eggs Benedict, marinated chicken breasts—" Their gazes met and locked over the last word. Nick's eyes dropped to Natalie's breasts, and he smiled, giving her that I-know-what-you-look-like-naked look. She felt her face grow warm.

"I didn't know women blushed anymore," Nick said.

"Only when they're in the company of dirty-minded, decadent—"

"I think I get your drift," Nick said, holding up both hands as though surrendering. "What do you recommend?"

"Therapy."

"To eat."

"The soup and salad is good."

"Suppose I'm hungry?"

"The club sandwich?"

Their waitress appeared. "Would you like a cocktail?"

Natalie shook her head. "We'll both have a Bloody Mary," Nick said. He glanced at Natalie. "C'mon, be a sport. How often do I get to come to Atlanta?"

She had been asking herself the same thing all morning.

Natalie sipped her drink slowly. The waitress served their salads and hurried away.

"What is this?" Nick asked, looking down at his salad.

"What is what?" Natalie looked at his bowl.

"This stuff that looks like somebody just weeded their garden and threw it on my salad."

"It's bean sprouts. Haven't you ever eaten them before?"

"Not while I was sober. Otherwise I'm sure I would have remembered. Is it just for decoration, or am I really supposed to eat it?"

"I shouldn't have brought you here. I should have taken you to the barbecue place downtown. Next time we'll go there."

He cocked a brow. "Next time?"

Natalie was at a loss for words. "Well, I just naturally assumed you'd visit your brother again sometime." Surely he wasn't going to go back to Cowpens and forget everything that had happened between them. What about his confession of love? Natalie's palms were damp. The thought of him leaving left an ache in her chest.

"What are you thinking about that has you looking so serious?" Nick asked.

She shrugged. "I was just wondering how soon you had to go back, that's all. There's a party tonight that I'm supposed to attend . . . one of the judges is retiring. A bunch of lawyers decided to send him and his wife on a seven-day cruise in the Caribbean."

"Nice retirement gift."

"I really should show up for a while since I helped plan the party. I would love you to go with me . . . if you wanted to, of course. We wouldn't have to stay long. I could wash your dress shirt and press your clothes when we get back to my place." She took a bite of her salad. She hadn't felt this nervous since she'd invited Donnie Banks to the Sadie Hawkins dance in tenth grade.

Nick smiled. "I'll go. I kind of like the idea of you doing my laundry and ironing my clothes."

Natalie returned the smile. "Don't be cocky. If there were time, your clothes would be sent to the dry cleaners."

"And here I thought you were getting domestic on me."

"Get serious," she replied. "I pay a lady to do that sort of thing."

They spent the afternoon sight-seeing, and decided to drop by Atlanta's impressive Peachtree Plaza for an exotic drink. Nick chose to take the outside glass-enclosed elevator to the top of the skyscraper, much to Natalie's horror. The elevator skimmed the outside of the building, offering a breathtaking view of the city.

"Is that the new Marriot over there?" Nick glanced around and frowned. "Natalie, what are you doing?"

"Praying," she mumbled, facing the metal doors, literally willing them to open and let her out.

"Aren't you going to look at the view?" Nick asked, tapping her on the shoulder.

She was thankful there was only one other couple in the elevator. "No. And if I ever get out of this thing, I'm going to wring your neck. I can't believe I let you talk me into riding in this contraption. Are we almost at the top?"

"We still have a couple of hundred feet to go," he said, watching her pale at his words.

"Lord, how *are* we going to get down?"

"I'm sure they have an inside elevator for the squeamish," he said, chuckling. "If not, I'll make sure you're very drunk before I put you back in this one."

"I would have to be comatose, Nick Jordan, before anybody could get me in this thing again." Natalie sighed her relief when the elevator came to a stop and the doors slid open with a whisper. She was the first one out. She grasped a metal rail. "I'm dizzy."

Nick saw there were tiny beads of perspiration on her upper lip. He was thankful when the hostess hurried over to seat them. "We don't care to sit next to the window," he said. The lady simply nodded and led them to a table beside a wall. "How's this?" he asked Natalie.

"Fine." Her voice was shaky.

"What do you want to drink?"

"Something potent. What do you suggest?"

"I thought we came here to get something exotic," he reminded her.

"As long as it'll stop my knees from knocking."

A cocktail waitress appeared, and Nick placed the order. "Two piña coladas," he said. "And would you tell the bartender to put a large slice of pineapple on each glass? We're pretending we're in the Bahamas."

The waitress smiled as she scribbled down the order. "So how come you're wearing your coats?" she asked matter-of-factly.

Nick didn't hesitate. "They lost our luggage on the plane coming over." The woman shot him a sympathetic look before she walked away.

"Your face is a light shade of green," Nick told Natalie.

"It is not." Natalie opened her purse and grabbed her compact. "Okay, maybe a tinge," she admitted, looking in the mirror.

"I understand this floor revolves so you can get a full view of Atlanta. Look, I can see the stadium."

"Good for you."

"Natalie, if you'd just relax, you might enjoy the sights."

"Next time bring an eagle."

Nick grinned. "Actually I'm enjoying this. I was beginning to think Natalie Courtland wasn't afraid of anything."

"I don't like deep snow, remember?"

"Or cold showers." Their eyes met briefly. It was obvious they were thinking about the first time Nick had kissed her. He gave her one of his wicked grins.

Natalie fidgeted self-consciously until their drinks arrived. She slurped her piña colada as though it were a milk shake. Finally she loosened the death grip on her chair. "So," she said after a moment, starting to feel a bit more relaxed, "I suppose you don't have many skyscrapers in Cowpens." When Nick shook his head, she thought for a moment. "Wonder why they named it Cowpens?"

"Because there were so many cowpens in the town," he said with a crooked smile. "Why'd they name this place Atlanta?"

" 'Cause Margaret Mitchell thought it sounded nice in her book, *Gone with the Wind*," she said, grinning. Actually she was starting to feel pretty good—as long as she didn't look toward the windows. She kept her gaze glued to Nick's face.

"I think you'd better slow down on that drink," he warned. "It may look like a vanilla milk shake, but I'm sure it's loaded with alcohol."

"Why do you think I'm guzzling it? I'm trying to work up the nerve to ride that elevator back to earth. I think after three or four more—"

"There's an inside elevator across from the bar."

She set down her drink. "Thank heaven. May we leave now?"

Once Nick had paid the check, they made their way in the direction of the inside elevator. Nick ushered Natalie in without saying a word. When they reached the ground level, she sighed her immense relief. "Next time you want to sit among the stars, take an airplane."

Nick laughed and hugged her against him. "I have stars in my eyes every time I'm with you."

They soon arrived at Natalie's condo, and she

put Nick's shirt in the wash right away. Then she went in search of him and found him stretched out on the bed. She sat beside him and brushed a strand of hair from his forehead, then wished she hadn't. The change of clothes he'd brought with him looked nothing like what he'd worn on the peach farm. The slacks were stylish, as was the shirt that stretched across his wide chest. It opened at the collar temptingly, just enough to show several brown sprigs of hair. "Tired?"

"Hmm."

"Is that a yes or a no?"

He reached for her and pulled her on top of him. One by one he unfastened the white buttons on her blouse, smiling at her in a way that made her pulse quicken. His eyes took in the lacy bra as he exposed it with deliberate slowness. "Not too tired," he said.

Natalie literally tingled with anticipation as Nick removed her clothes, enjoying how he took time to caress or press warm lips against each spot he bared. When she lay naked before him, the look in his eyes stole her breath away.

"Undress me."

Natalie hesitated. She had never undressed a man in her life—and it was broad daylight. She suddenly felt self-conscious.

As though reading her thoughts, Nick hooked a finger beneath her chin and raised it. "We have nothing to hide from each other," he said. "I'm not going to let you climb beneath the covers, lady. I adore every single inch of you, even that birthmark on your thigh."

Natalie blushed. "It's ugly. I've thought of having it removed."

"It's sexy as hell. Just thinking about it makes
me want you." As if to prove his point, he took
her hand and pressed it against his slacks. The
smile he gave her was brazen and filled with promise. "See what I mean?"

Natalie's fingers trembled slightly as she unbuttoned his shirt, but she was rewarded with the
sight of his handsome chest. She slid her fingers
through the coarse hair and buried her face against
it, inhaling the scent of his body. Nick helped her
by shrugging off the shirt, his gaze never leaving
her face.

The belt buckle and zipper on his slacks came
next. Natalie laughed at her ineptness. Once she
managed to get them open, Nick raised his hips
off the bed so she could pull down the slacks. She
folded them and laid them on a chair, then removed his socks and gazed at him.

"You're beautiful, Nick," she said without hesi-
tation. "I never thought a man could be beautiful." From his wide shoulders and chest to his flat
stomach he was a desirable man. His thighs were
hard and slightly muscular, as were his calves,
both covered with dark brown hair. There wasn't
an extra ounce on his body. Slowly she pulled
down the waistband of his underwear, exposing
his hardness. Her breath caught in her throat as
she gazed at him. She touched him lightly, tentatively, and heard his sigh of pleasure.

Nick sucked in his breath sharply when he felt

her lips on him. When he could stand no more, he gently pushed her away and sought to pleasure her in the same fashion. They made love tenderly, each content to study the lines and contours of the other's body, to find the erogenous points. Nick tongued the back of Natalie's knees until she squirmed, then nipped his way up her thighs. When he pulled her on top and entered her, Natalie thought she'd die from the rapture. Then he began moving his hips in a sensual motion that created friction against the heart of her desire. As the heat spread and shattered into a thousand starbursts of delight, Natalie trembled in his arms and cried out his name. His climax followed with a force that shook him to the core.

Afterward Nick stroked her lovingly. "I knew you'd be a tigress in bed. You may give other people the impression you're strictly business, but I knew once I got you in bed, I'd discover another side of you."

Natalie smiled lazily. "I hope that's a compliment."

"Damn right it is."

Nick was caught up in his thoughts. He couldn't believe his luck at finding someone as truly beautiful as the woman beside him. What caused the deep V between his brows was the question of what they were going to do about their feelings. Natalie would never be content to give up her hard-earned career and become a peach farmer's wife. And he would never ask her. On the other hand, he couldn't see himself joining forces with his brother in the investment business. He had built a life around his peach farm and cannery, just as Natalie had built hers fighting court battles.

His sigh was deep, coming from his very soul. He had known disappointment in love before, even sorrow, but losing Natalie would be more than he could bear. The thought of another man having her made him grit his teeth in rage. Something primitive inside told him she was his woman. He wanted to share the cold nights with her. He wanted to be the man to fill her belly with babies. Yet he knew that in time she would grow bored with her life and hate him.

Natalie snuggled in Nick's arms, giving a sigh of sheer pleasure. When his lips touched her hair, she looked up. "Are you tired?" she asked, her face still flushed from their lovemaking.

"No. I just want to lie here and hold you."

She lifted herself up on her elbow and kissed him gently on the lips. "I love you, Nick Jordan. Not only for saving my life but for giving me a new one." She smiled coyly. "And for being so darn good in bed."

"What do you mean by giving you a new life?" he asked, looking confused.

She lay her head in the crook of his shoulder and placed her hand on his wide chest. "I never thought I could be close to anybody again," she confessed. "I certainly never thought I could fall in love."

He was curious. "Why?"

She really didn't feel like going though the spiel, but she had to make him understand how he'd changed her life in so little time. "Well, when my mother left, I thought it was my fault. Then when Bobby died—" She let the sentence drop, not wanting to spoil the mood.

Nick knew the pain must have been horrendous. "I'm sorry you had to go through that," he said gently.

"I was consumed with anger at first. I felt I should have died alongside Bobby. I felt I didn't have a right to live."

"That happens sometimes," Nick said. "When I was in 'Nam, I had to carry my dead buddies back to the unit so their bodies could be shipped home. After a while I began to wonder why I was still alive. I felt guilty as hell at times."

Natalie nodded. "Sometimes I would find myself hating Bobby for what he did to me. He wasn't suffering anymore, but I was engulfed in pain. I began to wonder who was worse off." She and Nick gazed at each other. His look was tender. He understood.

"Well, now that we've got that off our chests, I suppose we should get ready for the party." They both laughed. Natalie felt good to be alive. Her senses had heightened; she had begun seeing things through new eyes, and she owed it to Nick. She knew how he must have suffered over Me Lin, but she refused to ask him about it. If the time came when he wanted to tell her, she would listen. It was hard for her knowing Nick had loved another woman and had had a child with her, but she would learn to live with it.

Natalie and Nick showered together, each enjoying soaping the other's body. Natalie ran her hands across his wide back and taut hips. She wondered if she would ever tire of looking at his body. Nick shampooed her hair, and Natalie felt as though her legs would fold beneath her. She closed her eyes and heard him chuckle.

"I think I've finally tamed my little tigress. All I have to do is stroke you or rub you to make you purr like a kitten."

"And what happens when I stroke you?" she asked with a saucy smile on her face.

He kissed the back of her neck. "It depends on the area you stroke."

They decided they would drive Natalie's Jaguar to the party, and she tossed Nick the keys. "I want you to take a test drive. One day the Blue Goose is going to bite the dust, and you'll have to buy something built in this century."

Nick couldn't help but respect the power and unique design of the car that reeked of class. It coasted along the road as though it weren't touching the asphalt. Maybe it *was* time he bought a new vehicle, he thought. He was beginning to spend more money on repairs to the Blue Goose than he would on a monthly car payment. Still, he didn't care for the flashiness of a Jaguar or Mercedes. Perhaps he'd buy a Blazer or a Jeep.

When Nick caught sight of the mansion on the hill, he was thankful they'd decided not to bring his truck. The last thing he wanted to do was embarrass Natalie in front of her colleagues.

Nick let out a low whistle as they got closer to the white house with its tall columns and stately veranda. "I didn't know judges made that kind of money. Does this guy accept bribes?"

Natalie laughed. "No, his wife comes from money. Old money," she added. "She can trace her ancestry all the way back to the Civil War. In fact, she usually does it at every social event."

"That should give us something to look forward to," he said, searching for a parking space. He finally found one and pulled into it. He shut off the engine and looked at Natalie. "Do we have to stay long?"

She looked surprised. "Not if you don't want to. Why?"

"Because you're so damn gorgeous tonight, I don't want to share you with anybody. And I don't want men looking at you in that thing you call a dress."

"This thing happens to be the in style now," she said, glancing down at her glittering blue tube dress. It was tight and strapless and short. She had bought it on a dare while shopping with one of the women from the office. It had remained on a hanger in her closet, and she'd been sure she had wasted good money buying it. Nick Jordan had given her a reason to wear it. Some part of her was determined to keep him wanting her.

Nick cradled Natalie's elbow in his palm as they made their way up the steps to the brightly lit mansion. Every once in a while he caught the scent of her perfume and thought it would make him crazy. If her perfume didn't, her dress surely would. When she had first slipped it on, he'd thought his eyes were going to pop out. The material molded to her body like a second skin, revealing each and every curve. The flat blue sequins were sewn together in a way that made her look as though she were wearing the skin of some reptile, which was even more thought provoking. Her hair was styled in a slightly mussed look, as though she had just climbed out of a man's bed—which in fact she had. The color of the dress matched her eyes and seemed to have the same fire each time the light touched it in a certain way. He liked it. It made him want to say to hell with the party, find a private place, and peel the garment away. He almost chuckled aloud at the vision of her wearing such a dress to a social event in Cowpens.

Natalie paused at the bottom of the steps of the elegant home and covered her mouth with one hand as though something were terribly wrong.

Nick frowned. "What's the matter?"

"Oh, Nick, don't let me bend over too far tonight," she whispered anxiously, her eyes wide in horror.

He blinked. "Why?"

Natalie glanced around to make sure she wasn't overheard. She looked stricken. "I was in such a hurry, I forgot to put on my panties!"

He swallowed, but his Adam's apple lodged in his throat. It was obvious he was at a loss as to what to do. "Aren't you wearing those things?

You know, pantyhose?" he asked, glancing at the slight sheen on her shapely legs.

"Yes, but they're pure silk. You can see right through them." He paled, and Natalie forced herself to keep from laughing. Her ploy had worked. Nick Jordan wasn't going to take his mind off her tonight.

"Should we leave?"

Natalie shook her head and sighed heavily. "It's too late for that. I'll just have to be careful."

Nick frowned. Careful hell. The dress was too short to begin with. He could just imagine her bending over . . . Aw, damn. He wasn't going to be able to think straight. He watched the gentle sway of her hips as she climbed the steps in front of him. Beads of sweat popped out on his forehead and upper lip.

It was going to be a long evening.

The party was in full swing as they entered the foyer. Natalie stopped several times to introduce Nick, but it was almost impossible to hear over the noise. Nick, with his mind still on Natalie's panties or lack thereof, headed straight for the bar. "Southern Comfort," he said. "Make it a double."

Natalie stood close beside him, so close her breast touched his sleeve. "I'll just have a club soda," she said, noting the pained expression on his face. She felt a little guilty for the prank she'd pulled.

Once they'd been served, Natalie led Nick outside to the pool area, where a jazz band was playing. She made a point of introducing Nick to everyone she knew, hoping to make him feel comfortable. "Oh, there's my father," she said.

Nick almost choked on his drink. "Your father?"

"Yes, come meet him." She slipped her arm through his and led him over to a tall man with salt and pepper hair wearing what looked to be a six-hundred-dollar suit. "Dad." Natalie tapped her father on the shoulder, and he turned around.

"Nat, I didn't see you come in," the older man said.

"We've just arrived. Dad, I'd like you to meet Nick Jordan from Cowpens, South Carolina. Nick, this is my father, Lamar Courtland."

"Not *the* Nick Jordan," her father said, pumping Nick's hand. "Are you the one who dug my daughter out of all that snow?"

"He's the one," Natalie said proudly.

"Well, it's a pleasure to meet you," Lamar Courtland said. " I don't suppose I can thank you enough for saving my daughter's life. My law firm couldn't make it without her. I guess you've heard she's hailed as the toughest divorce attorney in Atlanta." He glanced at Natalie. "Don't you look nice tonight. I'm glad to see you've gone a little flashy. Those business suits and glasses you wear all the time are never going to get you a husband." He didn't notice the blush on her face. "Would you two excuse me? I just saw an old friend of mine." He hurried away without another word.

"Well, that's my father," Natalie said dully, still embarrassed by his remark about finding a husband.

Nick watched the man walk away. So that was her father. No wonder she had clung to her brother.

". . . And this is Rick and Julie Robbins. Rick, Julie, meet Nick Jordan," Natalie said, introducing him to a couple who'd been walking past.

Nick shook hands with both of them. He'd been introduced to so many people, he knew he'd never remember their names. "Nice to meet you," he said, having said those exact words at least a hundred times. He was bored and ready to leave.

"Rick and Julie have their own law firm," Natalie said.

Nick tried to look interested. "Really?"

"Do you practice in the Atlanta area, Nick?" Rick asked.

"Nick isn't an attorney."

"I'm a peach farmer," Nick stated flatly.

"How interesting," Julie said in a tone that suggested otherwise. "I don't think I've ever met a peach farmer."

"Actually Nick is being a bit modest," Natalie cut in. "Not only does he own half the land in the town of Cowpens, but he employs hundreds of people in his cannery."

Julie looked impressed. "You have your own cannery?"

"Would you excuse me?" Nick asked, walking away from them abruptly, unaware of the shocked looks he'd been given. He exited through the front door and made his way down the steps. He took a seat on the bottom step and sipped his drink quietly. Several minutes later he heard the sound of high heels behind him.

"Nick, what's wrong?" Natalie asked. "Aren't you enjoying yourself?"

"How do you know so much about my farm and the cannery?" he asked angrily.

The question surprised her. "Your brother told me. Why?"

"Just curious," he said, wondering why it irked him that she knew about his financial standing. "When you were staying at my place, you shuddered every time I touched you. Now you can't get enough." He towered over her when he stood. "Was it my money that coaxed you into bed with me?"

Natalie was so taken aback by the question that she couldn't gather her thoughts for a moment. When she did, she was angry—mad as hell, to be exact. "Are you accusing me of being a gold digger?" she asked between gritted teeth. "Because if you are, let me remind you, Nick Jordan, that I do very well on my own. I don't need your money. In fact, I don't need a damn thing from you. I'm perfectly capable of taking care of myself."

"So I've noticed." He looped his thumb over his belt. "You know, if you work at it long enough, you'll be the spittin' image of your father. Now, *that's* something to look forward to, isn't it?"

In a rage, Natalie raised her hand to slap his face. He caught her by her wrist and held it painfully. "Don't even think about it. I'm not the gentleman your cohorts pretend to be. I may just slap you back."

She gritted her teeth. "You're the type who would. You obviously have no manners."

He glared at her for a moment before releasing her. "You're right. While most of these jerks were learning their manners at Harvard," he said in a mocking tone, "I was fighting their damn war. You think they're so smart. Go in and ask a few of them if they even know what Vietnam was about. Odds are, they were partying while the rest of us were crawling through mosquito-infested swamps." He turned on his heel and made his way down the sidewalk.

"Just where do you think you're going?" Natalie demanded.

"I'll wait for you in the car."

Natalie remained at the party only long enough to watch someone present the judge and his wife with their gift. She felt miserable. To make matters worse, several men had openly flirted with her. She would burn the dress. The judge made a brief speech and everyone clapped. Natalie slipped out the front door and located the car. Nick was waiting just as he'd promised.

The drive to her apartment was made in silence. Nick's jaw was tense, and his gaze never left the road. When he pulled into Natalie's parking space, he helped her out of the car and walked quietly into her building. Once inside her apartment, he headed straight for the bedroom. Natalie followed and found him stuffing his extra clothes into the small suitcase he'd brought with him.

"What are you doing?"

He didn't look up. "That should be obvious. I'm leaving."

Natalie stood rooted to the spot. Fear welled up in her chest. "Nick, I was only trying to take up for you in front of that snob Julie Robbins."

Nick raised to his full height. His eyes were distant and cold. "Why should you have to defend me in front of anybody? I don't owe anybody an explanation, especially some woman I've never laid eyes on."

"Why do you insist on acting like a poor country boy? What's so bad about admitting you're a successful farmer and businessman?"

"Because that's exactly what I was when I came back from Vietnam. Dirt poor. My parents were in hock to their kneecaps. I tried to sell the place to cover the debts, but nobody wanted a worthless peach farm. Not even my brother and sister." He paused as though remembering. "I busted my rear to get it running, fighting crop diseases I'd never heard of. That and a little luck turned the place into a success. It didn't happen overnight. The only reason I built the cannery was to give local people desperately needed jobs. I had no way of knowing it would be so profitable."

"And you really don't give a damn, do you?"

"No, I really don't. I guess it has something to do with priorities. I feel lucky to be alive. I'm healthy, I have enough to eat. That's really all that matters. I don't have to flaunt my success. People seem to like me the way I am."

"I'm not flaunting my success. But I refuse to

work twelve hours a day, then shop at the Salvation Army for my wardrobe."

Nick stood there for a moment, looking at her, wanting to plant the memory of her face in his mind forever. "You're the most beautiful woman I've ever met."

The change in conversation startled her. "You're leaving," she said dully. Her eyes burned with unshed tears.

"I have to. There are too many things we can't change about ourselves, Natalie. I can't handle this kind of life." A single tear slid down her cheek, and it broke his heart. He wanted to take her in his arms and kiss away the pain that he himself was causing. "It's not just you, Natalie. It's me." He raked his hands through his hair. "When I was in 'Nam, we were taught to spread out while stalking the enemy. If we walked in groups, we were easy targets, but if we walked alone, we had a better chance of making it."

"So what has that got to do with us?" she asked, trying to swallow a sob.

"When I first got back to the States, I couldn't even walk into a grocery store or sit in a theater. Crowds scared the hell out of me. The only place I felt safe was among the peach trees on my parents' farm."

"But you were in a crowd tonight and a restaurant last night."

"I've overcome most of my fears. But I could never live in a city this large. The traffic and the people would suffocate me. And look at us. I don't have anything in common with your friends. I don't know the first thing about law or art, and the subject of politics bores me. I don't drive a Mercedes or wear five-hundred-dollar suits."

"But you could afford to."

"That's the point. I don't want it. And for some reason you don't seem to understand that."

"That's a cop-out, Nick Jordan, and you know it," Natalie said, putting her hands on her hips. "I couldn't care less that you don't know anything about art or law, because I don't know a damn thing about peaches, and frankly I could spend the rest of my life ignorant on the subject. It's an excuse. You're not walking out on me because we're different. You're leaving because you're scared."

"Of what?"

"You're still mourning Me Lin and the baby, aren't you? Even after all these years you blame yourself for their deaths. Well, you haven't exactly cornered the market on heartache. I've lost out too. But these past couple of days with you have shown me I can be happy again. I know what it's like to love again."

Nick felt saddened for both of them as he closed the suitcase and walked out of the bedroom to the front door. He glanced once more at Natalie and saw a look of devastation on her face. He couldn't bear it. "I love you, Natalie. Try to be happy." He opened the door and walked out.

Natalie stood for a long time looking at the door, hoping and praying that Nick would walk back in and everything would be okay between them. Sure they lived different lives, but couldn't they work something out? How many times had she asked her clients the same question? Yet neither she nor Nick would give an inch.

You always lose the people you love. She moved like a statue, turning off lights, locking her door. In the bedroom she slipped out of her dress and tossed it onto the floor. She pulled down the sheets and climbed beneath them.

She didn't cry until she caught Nick's scent on the pillow beside her. When the sobs came, it was like a floodgate opening. She cried for her mother, for Bobby, and for the love she'd never gotten from her father.

Not only had Nick Jordan made her fall in love with him—he'd made her take a good look at herself. She didn't like what she saw.

Ten

Natalie sipped her first cup of coffee of the morning and gazed down from the small patio table on her balcony at the activity below. A street cleaner chugged along the curb, its giant circular brushes cleaning away the night's debris.

When the elegant French-style telephone rang in the living room a moment later, Natalie frowned. She wasn't ready to talk to anybody yet, after having spent another sleepless night. She would be tired and irritable the rest of the day. The last thing she needed was a call from a hysterical client at six-thirty in the morning. She sighed and reached for the phone. The coffee cup almost slipped from her fingers when she heard Nick Jordan's voice.

"I just wanted to see how you were doing," he said hurriedly from the other end of the line as though half afraid she might hang up. "And to apologize for being such a jerk the other night."

All of Natalie's defenses drifted into thin air. "There's no need to apologize," she said, at the same time trying to remain aloof. "Everything you said was true." That's what hurt. Not only had Nick walked out on her, he had forced her to take personal inventory. He had seen through her facade so easily. Atlanta's hottest divorce lawyer was nothing but a lonely, insecure woman who hid behind expensive clothes, a flashy car, and a six-figure condominium.

"I had no right to say those things to you, Natalie. Lord knows I've enough problems of my own. I never meant to hurt you." He paused briefly. "I want to be your friend. I want you to know I'm here if you need me."

"Friend?" she asked, testing the word on her tongue. She almost laughed aloud. How could she be mere friends with a man whom she'd made love to with reckless abandon? She had tasted his body, sought out the crevices and pleasure points with her lips and tongue until she was rewarded with sighs of gratification. In her mind she could still remember his distinctive scent. She had shared an intimacy with him she'd never known with another man.

And now he expected her to be his friend?

"What we had was wonderful, Natalie. The best. I know I'll never find it with another woman."

"But it isn't enough," she said to him as much as to herself. She could feel a lump growing at the back of her throat. Why had he called? Why had he forced her to remember things she had tried to forget these past few days, even though the memories played in her mind every night like an old rerun as she tried to sleep.

"I'll be your friend, Nick," she said dully. "After all, you saved my life."

"I don't want gratitude," he said harshly.

"Then what *do* you want?" She had raised her voice but she didn't care. There was silence on the other end of the line. Her eyes teared. "I have to go, Nick—"

"Wait!" He paused, not knowing what to say but wanting to keep her on the line as long as possible. He had missed hearing her voice, her laughter, hcr whispers of delight during their lovemaking. "If you need anything . . . anything at all—"

Silent tears slid down her cheeks. "You know how resilient I am," she said. "I'll be fine." When she hung up the tclephone a few seconds later, she buried her face in her hands and cried. Damn the man! Why had he made her fall in love with him? Her mind whirled relentlessly, just as the snow had the night he'd pulled her out of its deadly grasp.

Over the next couple of weeks Natalie understood why Pinocchio had yearned to be a real live boy instead of a wooden puppet. That's how she felt, wooden and lifeless. And like a puppet, she made all the motions, as though someone else were pulling the strings. She came to work each day, answered telephone calls, met with clients, and made court appearances. She tried to feel sympathetic toward those who sought her professional help, but her heart had obviously turned to wood as well. If people thought her cold and distant, it was just as well. A newspaper article had once referred to her as the courtroom she-devil. Perhaps she was merely living up to her reputation.

When Natalie arrived home each night, usually after staying late at the office, she often found herself standing in the doorway studying the living room, trying to see it through Nick's eyes. No wonder he hadn't wanted to sit on the sofa. The furniture literally smelled of money. She and her decorator had worked for hours with paint, paper, and fabric to get just the right look. Unfortunately, the room resembled the lobby of a hotel more than a *living* room.

The answering machine was blinking when she checked it, but there were no messages. All her clients left messages, she thought. Had Nick called again? What did he want, for heaven's sake? Was he so guilt stricken that he felt she'd hurl herself over the balcony after the way they'd parted? Stop it, she told herself. Stop thinking about him. But her efforts were futile as thoughts of him invaded her dreams again that night.

One morning Guy Pressman bounced into her office unannounced and planted himself on the corner of her desk. "Good morning, beautiful."

Natalie didn't look up. "Go away," she muttered. "I don't have time to play with you today."

Guy raised both brows. "I'm genuinely hurt, Nat. Here I decide to walk with you to the courthouse, entertain you with my charm and—"

Natalie gave him a bored look. "Why should I

want to walk to the courthouse? I practically live there as it is."

Guy looked surprised. "Does the name Evelyn St. James versus Melvin St. James ring a bell?"

Natalie froze in her seat. "That's today?"

Guy checked his wristwatch. "In less than half an hour to be exact."

Natalie grabbed the computer printout that listed her schedule each day. The St. James divorce case was set for nine o'clock. "Oh, no!" She rushed from her chair to one of three filing cabinets. "I haven't looked at that file in weeks."

Natalie couldn't find the folder. She bumped her knee on the drawer and tore a hole in her silk stockings. "Dammit, Carla, get in here!" Her secretary, obviously shocked at Natalie's tone of voice, came running.

"What is it?" the woman asked, her eyes scanning the room as though she expected to find it on fire.

"I can't find the St. James file." Natalie sounded desperate. "I have to be in court in twenty minutes, and I don't even know if I've filed all the motions with the clerk's office."

Her secretary was already opening and closing drawers to the file cabinet. "I'm sure you have. I've never known you to be remiss about things like that."

Until she'd fallen in love, Natalie thought.

"Here," Carla said calmly, handing it over.

"Where was it?" Natalie's tone bordered on hysteria.

"It was misfiled. That temp we hired is always

losing files. Fortunately, I've picked up on her system."

"I want her fired immediately!" Natalie said, realizing she was trembling. "I can't have some nit-wit screwing up my files. Call the agency and get someone qualified."

Carla looked surprised. "But, Nat—"

"I don't have time to argue," Natalie said, waving the folder in the air as she walked around her desk and sat down. "I've got to go over this file. Guy, go out in the lobby and watch the goldfish swim or something until I'm ready."

Guy gave her a long look. "On second thought, I think I'll let you walk to the courthouse alone." He got up from the desk and sauntered out the door.

For a moment Natalie was stunned. "What's wrong with him?" she asked Carla.

Carla shrugged. "How should I know? I'm still trying to figure out what's wrong with you. If you need me, feel free to yell at the top of your lungs." She closed the door behind her.

Natalie stared at the closed door. Had she really been that difficult to work with for the past week or so? The last thing she wanted to do was hurt the people she respected and cared about. She had known Guy for more than five years, and Carla had been her secretary from the beginning.

"Oh, damn," she muttered under her breath. She'd have to apologize to both of them. But right now she didn't have a moment to spare as she opened the St. James file and began scanning the pages.

Five minutes later Natalie leaned back in her

chair and sighed. Everything was in order. Everything, that was, except her life.

Nick walked through the rows of peach trees, where an early morning mist hung in the air and clung to the branches. Daisy walked beside him, having nursed her pups until their bellies were full and they'd become drowsy. Nick had been up since before dawn. As always, his thoughts during the night had centered on Natalie. He thought of her lying in her own pristine bed in Atlanta, and his gut had wrenched with desire.

Nick stopped to examine the leaves on one tree. It would not blossom until mid-March, but at least it looked as though he was going to have a crop after all.

As if he gave a damn. The whole orchard and cannery could go straight to hell for all he cared. Without Natalie beside him to share his work and life, it mattered little. He turned for the house, bored with the orchard and life in general. Once inside, he drank another cup of coffee and debated whether to call Natalie before she left for the office. What was the use? he thought. It would only serve as a catalyst to open their wounds. He would wait until she left for work, then call, just so he could hear her lovely voice on the answering machine.

Then, as usual, he would hang up.

Nick had done a lot of thinking over the past couple of weeks. He had never believed there would be happiness in life after Vietnam. He had more or less reconciled himself to living in the large house alone, hiring and firing men to tend his crop and making sure only the best peaches made it to the cannery. Now he realized he'd merely been going through the motions of living.

Until Natalie.

He hadn't worked in the cannery or done the numerous tasks that kept him busy on the farm much of the time since he'd walked out of Natalie's apartment.

Part of him wanted to drive to Atlanta and drag her back with him. But he knew caveman tactics would never work with her. She'd probably have him arrested for kidnapping. But he knew she loved him, dammit! And he worshiped every gorgeous inch of her. There had to be a way.

Natalie finished up early one day and was on her way out the door when she spotted a woman and two small children sitting in the lobby. Although the woman looked frail, she held both children in her lap.

"Is someone helping you?" Natalie asked, seeing the weary look in the woman's eyes.

"I was told to wait," she answered. "I been waiting since after lunch, but I don't reckon anybody will have time to see me today. I—I heard there was a good lawyer here who did divorces, so I just took the bus and here I am."

Natalie noted the worn shoes the woman and the children wore. She didn't think the woman could afford their next meal, much less the ser vices of Lamar Courtland's firm. "What's your name?" Natalie asked gently.

"Naomi. Naomi Patterson. These are my kids, Barton and Cindy."

Natalie wrestled with indecision. "Mrs. Patterson, why don't you come into my office?" She didn't miss the look of astonishment on the receptionist's face as they made their way down the hall.

"Carla, this is Mrs. Patterson," Natalie said as soon as she stepped into her secretary's office. "We need to discuss some business in my office. Would you be a dear and take the children to the lounge and see what we have in the refrigerator?"

"Of course," Carla said brightly, giving Natalie a look that told her she'd summed up the situation immediately.

"James drinks," Naomi said once they were in the privacy of Natalie's office. "He has for years. Then he gets mean."

"Can you prove it?"

Mrs. Patterson unbuttoned her dress to her waist and pulled it off. Natalie gasped aloud when she saw the black and blue marks. "I have some bruises in other places."

"You know I'll have to have pictures for evidence if you want to retain me," Natalie said, feeling nothing but pity for the woman.

"I have only fifty dollars," she said, stuffing her arms back in the sleeves of her dress. "I been taking a dollar or two from the grocery money each week."

"Do you have anywhere to go?"

The woman nodded. "My family will come get

me, but it won't do no good if I don't divorce James. He'll drag me back home."

Natalie handed Naomi a clipboard. "Just fill out the top portion so we can start on this right away. I have a friend who runs a shelter for women who have problems like yours. You can stay there until your family comes for you." Once Naomi had filled out the form, Natalie took it and picked up the microphone to her Dictaphone. "Carla, I want you to type a petition for divorce on grounds of physical and mental cruelty and habitual drunkenness. I'd like to request an emergency divorce on the same grounds. Also, get me a restraining order. I don't want this man to ever lay hands on his wife again. Request the judge to deny the husband visitation with his children until he seeks counseling and puts a stop to the drinking. I recommend an anger-control group and A.A."

Once Natalie got what pertinent information she needed, she ejected the tape and stood. "Your papers will be filed with the clerk's office tomorrow." She dialed her friend's number at the shelter, then informed Naomi someone would be there to pick them up within half an hour.

Naomi had tears in her eyes as she reached into her purse and pulled out a roll of money held together with a rubber band. "This is all I can pay right now, but once I get a job—"

"Keep it for the children," Natalie said. "I have enough rich clients to keep the place running."

"God bless you, Miss Courtland."

Natalie led the woman to the lounge for a cup of coffee until her ride came. She saw that Carla had given the children packs of crackers and soft drinks. At least it would tide them over. She was ready to leave when Carla buzzed her.

"Natalie, there's an Arthur Jordan on line two for you."

Natalie frowned. "Who?"

"He says he's Nick Jordan's brother."

"Oh," she said wearily.

"He says it's important."

Natalie stiffened, praying nothing had happened to Nick. "Okay, I'll take it." She pushed her speaker button. "Mr. Jordan, how can I help you?" she asked, using her professional voice.

"Nice hearing your voice again, Miss Courtland. Is the law practice keeping you busy these days?"

"Extremely busy," she said in case he was calling for a dinner date. "What did you have on your mind, Mr. Jordan?"

"Call me Arthur," he insisted. "I just wanted to see if you were interested in a solid investment."

"I don't think so. I don't make a lot of investments, but when I do, I use my father's broker."

"Wait before you turn it down," Arthur cautioned. "There's a lot of money to be made in the canning business these days. Especially if you've got a reputation behind you."

"What kind of canning business?" Natalie cut in.

"Peaches."

"Not Nick's." She knew he'd never sell.

"Yes, ma'am. He's getting rid of the whole caboodle."

Natalie straightened in her chair. "What about the house and the orchard? Is he selling those too?"

"Well, that's not really my territory," Arthur said. "I believe he has a realtor working with him on that. But I've put together a couple of interested buyers for the cannery, if you think you'd like to get in on the action."

Natalie's ears were still ringing with the news. "Where's he going?"

"Beats me. You interested in the cannery?"

"Uh, let me get back to you, Arthur." Natalie hung up the telephone and jumped from her chair. She grabbed her purse and coat on the way out. "Did Mrs. Patterson get her ride?" Carla smiled and nodded. "I'm going to the library," Natalie said quickly.

"The what?"

"I don't expect to return." She left a confused secretary staring after her.

Natalie cursed the Atlanta traffic as she made her way to the downtown library. She weaved in and out of fast-moving cars, her mind preoccupied with what she had to do. The drive took unusually long, and Natalie was ready to pull her hair out by the time she reached the parking lot of the public library. Once inside, she made her way quickly to the reference section.

"Excuse me."

A woman with orange hair and horn-rimmed glasses looked up in boredom. "May I help you?" she asked in a voice that sounded as though it had been tape-recorded.

"Yes, please," Natalie said. "I would like to get some demographic data on a specific area."

Without a word the woman stood and walked

toward a shelf of books. "Okay, what d'you want to know?"

Lamar Courtland lumbered down the hall carrying his golf bag and clubs over one shoulder. He passed by Natalie's door, then stopped and backed up. "What's going on?"

"Hello, Dad. Come in and have a seat. Oh, would you please close the door?" Natalie added. Before he could respond, she went on. "Surely you're not playing golf in these temperatures. Can't you wait until it warms up?"

Her father leaned his golf bag against a shelf and closed the door. "I was just going to clean my clubs so I'm ready when the time comes." He took a seat in one of the leather chairs in front of Natalie's desk. "What are all these boxes doing in here?"

"I'm packing," she said simply.

Lamar Courtland merely stared at his daughter. "Packing?" he echoed. "Why? Are you going somewhere?" When she nodded, he straightened in his chair with a frown. "Has another firm offered you a better deal?"

Natalie continued to stack her law books into a cardboard box. She couldn't help but smile at her father's question. "No, Dad. In fact, I'm thinking of starting my own firm. If I get lonely, I'll find a partner, but—"

Lamar stood. "You can't do that!"

Natalie looked up calmly from her task. "Why not?"

It was obvious her father was dumbfounded. "We . . . I mean, I need you here. You're the best damn divorce lawyer we have."

Natalie folded her arms across her chest. Her look was challenging. "And what do you think of me as a daughter?"

Lamar looked baffled, an expression Natalie had never seen on her father's face. "As a daughter?" He recovered immediately. "You've been a wonderful daughter, never given me a minute's trouble. Always made straight A's. Any father would be proud."

Natalie felt her eyes sting with unshed tears. "But do you love me?"

"Nat, what's gotten into you, for Pete's sake? You've been working too hard. Why don't you fly to Barbados for a week?"

"I want to know if you love me . . . if you *ever* loved me."

"Of course I loved you!" he bellowed. "I'm your father, aren't I? I fed and clothed you, sent you to the best schools, gave you a job. What else could I have done for you?"

The tears slid down her cheek. "You could have just once told me you loved me, Dad." She reached for a tissue. "All these years I've wanted to hear it from you. Just once. First Mother left, then Bobby died. Do you realize I had nobody?"

Her father sank in the chair and rubbed the bridge of his nose with his thumb and forefinger. It was a long time before he spoke. When he did, his voice was broken and the lines on his face more noticeable. "Who the hell do you think had?" Natalie remained silent. "When your mother left, I thought I'd never survive it. Then Bobby—" He looked up apologetically and shook his head. "That was the final blow for me. I knew you needed me, but I had nothing left to give. That didn't mean I didn't love you . . . I just felt empty inside."

Natalie noticed that the rims of his eyes were red. She watched him stand and walk around to her side of the desk. He took both of her hands in his. "I *do* love you, Nat. I've always loved you."

Natalie stood and hugged him, knowing it was an awkward moment for him. She stepped back and gave him a tearful smile. "Thank you. I'm glad we got that straightened out."

He wiped his forehead. "I need a drink. Does this mean you'll stay?"

She shook her head. "Nothing personal. I just think I'd like to work for some real people for a while. Those who can't afford to step through the hallowed doors of the Courtland firm with a thousand dollars for a retainer. But don't worry, I've passed most of my cases to other attorneys."

"Where will you practice?"

"Have you ever heard of a town called Spartanburg, South Carolina? I did some checking, and it's a fair-size town. Located about seven miles from Cowpens."

"So this has something to do with that . . . uh, that—" He snapped his fingers several times as though hoping it would give him his answer.

"Peach farmer," Natalie supplied. "Yes, it does. He just doesn't know yet." She glanced down at her hands. "I just hope he'll have me."

"He will. If he's smart." Her father paused. "Anything I can do to help?"

"Just touch base with my realtor from time to time. I'm selling my condo. And take care of this one case for me," she added, handing him Naomi Patterson's file. "You won't make a dime, but it's very important to me. Promise?" Her father nodded.

"Aren't you moving kind of fast on this? I mean, what if it doesn't work out? You'll come back with no place to live."

Natalie smiled confidently. "Dad, when it feels this right, you know it's going to last."

Natalie's Jaguar ate up the white lines in the road as she sped toward Cowpens. Her stomach dipped briefly when she finally exited the interstate, but she tried to reassure herself that everything would be okay. She made several wrong turns on the back roads looking for Nick's house, but when she spotted it, she pressed the brakes and sat there. What if he didn't want her? What if she'd quit her job, listed her condo, and crammed her trunk and backseat with what she could, just to be rejected by Nick? Fear gripped her at the thought.

Natalie took a deep breath, drove the short distance to his house, and pulled into the driveway behind the Blue Goose. She couldn't help but smile. Some things never changed. No, that wasn't quite true, she thought, turning off the ignition. Feelings changed. She had rearranged her entire life in the hope that Nick still loved her. Suddenly she felt very foolish. Of course, the only way she would know how he felt was to ask him. She had spent much of her life craving love in silence. This time she would demand to know where she stood. Nick Jordan owed her that much.

Natalie knocked on the front door, feeling less courageous by the moment. After a minute she knocked again loudly, remembering that Nick spent most of his time in the back of the house. She was just about to go around to the back door when the knob turned and the front door opened.

She almost didn't recognize him. He just stared as though she were a vision. It was obvious he hadn't shaved in a week, and he looked gaunt. Her heart went out to him. When she spoke, her voice trembled. "May I come in, Nick?"

He raised his chin a fraction and studied her. "That depends on whether you plan to stay this time."

"I want to stay. If you'll have me." Natalie barely got the words out of her mouth before she was crushed against his wide chest. All at once Nick's lips were everywhere, in her hair, at her temples, on her forehead, and finally covering her mouth. He kissed her hungrily, his beard scratching her cheek. It was a wonderful sensation.

"I'm sorry, baby, my face must feel like sandpaper," he said once he broke the kiss. He caressed her cheek. "What am I thinking? You're standing out in the cold." Without warning he swept her up in his arms, kicked the front door closed, and carried her through the house to the den. He drank his fill of the sight of her as though half afraid she might slip away again.

Natalie laughed. "I can walk, Nick."

He settled himself on the couch with her on his lap. "Don't move. Just let me look at you. You're beautiful."

"So are you," she whispered, running a finger across his bottom lip. "I've missed you, Nick."

He groaned. "Darlin', if you've suffered half as much as I have . . . That's why I called your place every day . . . just to hear your voice on the answering machine."

"That was you hanging up all the time?"

"I didn't want to cause you any more pain than I already had. What's this under your coat, blue jeans?" He sounded surprised. "Lord, I love the way they grab your rear."

"I figured if I was going to live on a peach farm, I might as well dress for it."

He sobered instantly. "What about your career, Natalie?"

"I've already done some preliminary checking, and I think I'm going to open a small office in Spartanburg. I'm tired of dealing with the country-club set. And I'm tired of concentrating solely on divorce. Now, are you going to let me live here, or have you already sold the place?"

His brows bunched together in a frown. "Sold the place?"

"Yes. Your brother called me and said you'd listed the house and property with a realtor, and he wanted to know if I wanted to go in with some investors on the cannery, and why do I feel I've been had?"

"Arthur called you?"

"He told me you were selling out."

Nick shook his head. "I may have been disillusioned a couple of times, but I'd never sell the place."

It took several seconds before Natalie understood. "Your brother purposely tricked me into coming here!" she said hotly.

"Remind me to thank him," Nick said, nibbling her earlobe. Arthur had called several times to find him wallowing in self-pity, but Nick never thought his brother would go to such lengths to help him.

"I feel like an idiot."

"How would you like to feel like warm butter?" Nick stood with her in his arms and carried her into the bedroom. When he had her naked on the bed, he stripped his clothes off and joined her, his lips tracing every line and curve on her body. When she pleaded with him to take her, his thrust was powerful and took her breath away. Soon they were moving frantically against each other. Nick's mouth captured hers as Natalie whispered his name and shuddered in delight only a moment before he did. They lay together for a long time afterward, just enjoying the moment. Nick was the first to speak.

"Natalie, you can't just live here," he said simply.

Her heart sank. "Y—you don't want me?"

"Hell yes, I want you," he said, pulling her closer, "but not as my roommate. Besides, people in this part of the world frown on that sort of thing. This isn't Atlanta. Folks here are a bit old-fashioned."

"Nick, what are you saying? That I should get an apartment?"

He propped himself up on one elbow. "You know for someone who has had as much schooling as you, you're not real quick on the draw."

She was becoming irritated. "Meaning?"

"I'm trying to propose marriage to you, Natalie, for heaven's sake!"

She squealed in delight and began kissing his face in earnest. "You won't be sorry, Nick, I promise you."

He chuckled. "You make it sound as if I'm buying a hog." She punched him playfully, then lay back in his arms. "We're going to be so good together. We'll make love in front of the fireplace every night."

"I like the sound of that. Are there going to be any babies as a result of our campfire meetings?"

"Do you want one?" she asked hopefully. When he nodded, she hugged him tighter. "We'll have to have a nursery, of course. I think as my wedding present to you, I'll completely renovate the house."

"Are you going to choose the sofa?"

"No, *we're* going to choose the furniture together. Something you can sit on. I want to make this a home, not a showplace."

Nick's heart swelled with love at the radiant look on her face. "Let's get married right away. I want you to be my wife as soon as possible."

She nodded. "Me too."

The telephone rang on the nightstand. Nick groaned and answered it. "Oh, hello, Arthur."

"Give me the phone!" Natalie demanded. "I have something to say to that worm, that urchin."

Nick grinned and held the phone away from her. "Yes, she's here. I'll have to admit you did a good job. I owe you one, buddy." Nick hung up before Natalie could grab the phone from his hand.

"Were you in on Arthur's little trick?" she asked, crossing her arms and glaring at Nick. "Arthur wouldn't have taken the time to think up all that by himself. You *told* him to call me, didn't you?"

"Natalie, I'm surprised at you," Nick said, looking genuinely hurt. "Do you think I would try to manipulate you to get what I wanted?"

Natalie pondered the thought. His face was a mask of innocence. "No, I suppose not," she finally said, going back into his arms. "I'm sorry. Remember, I'm a lawyer. I'm just naturally suspicious."

"I forgive you, baby." Nick closed his eyes, contented to be next to the woman he loved. Tomorrow he would call Arthur's tailor and order several new suits. It was the least he could do.

Epilogue

Nick watched Natalie bite into the luscious peach, and a bit of the juice slid lazily down her chin. He smiled, stifling the urge to lick the nectar with his own tongue. As if guessing his thoughts, Natalie turned from the window. Lord, she looked as delectable as the fruit in her hand, he thought. And the nectar that her body yielded was twice as sweet.

"You're not eating your lunch," she said lovingly. Natalie had learned to read Nick's looks during the four months they'd been married. His eyes told her the last thing he had on his mind was ham and cheese. She swallowed a smile and reached down to pet Daisy and a male pup who stood by her side like a sentinel. Daisy had become Natalie's personal watchdog. It was as though the animal realized that Natalie was a permanent fixture in the household now. While good homes had been found for the other puppies once they'd been weaned, Natalie had insisted on keeping one male.

"I'm more interested in you," Nick said, gazing at his wife with heavy eyelids. Her fine blond hair had grown over the months into a flattering shoulder-length style that curled at the ends. There was color in her cheeks and a light tan on her bare arms from her daily treks through the orchards, which were alive with activity now. It was peach-picking season, and crews of men worked from sunup till sundown, clearing acres of trees. When Natalie wasn't working at her law office, she seemed to enjoy watching the workers. Once the peaches were picked, they were carefully packed into crates and loaded onto trucks, then driven to the cannery, where they were processed for market. All of Cowpens became involved in one way or another. Folks seemed to put everything on the back burner, as it was often said, until Nick Jordan's crop was ready for market. Luckily the snowstorm had done very little damage to the trees.

A cool June breeze blew through the window, fanning Natalie's hair from her face and flattening the baggy blouse against her expanding abdomen. Nick sucked in his breath at the sight. His child. She was carrying *his* child! Every time he thought about it he glowed with pride. When Natalie had first told him, only a month after their marriage, he hadn't slept a wink that night. All he could think of was their baby growing inside of her. He had wanted to tell the world. Instead, he told everyone in Cowpens. Although they hadn't

discussed it, he planned to be with her at the
birth. He would hold her hand through the entire
episode, and even though they planned to take
childbirth classes, he would insist that her doctor
not let her suffer. He wouldn't allow his wife to go
through pain no matter what he had to do. Be
sides, he was bigger than her doctor. He frowned
No, that wouldn't do. Natalie would never forgive
him if he belted her doctor in the delivery room.

"Have you had a nap yet?" he asked, biting into
the ham and cheese sandwich she'd prepared.

Natalie laughed, tossed the core of the peach
into the garbage can, and washed her hands. She
joined Nick at the table. "I'm not tired," she stated
flatly as she often did.

"Still . . ." He tried to look stern. "You need
your rest. The book says—"

"I wish you'd stop reading all those pregnanc
and baby books," she interrupted him. "You'r
starting to sound like my doctor."

"You're working too hard."

"Three days a week!" she shrieked. "I used t
average sixty hours a week in Atlanta."

"You weren't three months pregnant then." An
more beautiful than ever, he thought. "The firs
trimester is the most crucial."

"I know that, Nick. You told me yesterday. An
the day before that. But I want to keep activ
right up until the baby comes," she said. "I fe
useful by working."

He raised both brows. "Are you trying to tell m
you don't feel useful here?"

"There's a difference. When I'm representin

someone who wouldn't normally be able to afford an attorney, I feel as if I'm making a contribution to society. I know I'm not bringing in the big bucks the way I was in Atlanta, but it doesn't matter anymore. Does that sound dumb?"

Nick saw in her eyes that his opinion truly mattered. He reached across the table and took one slender hand in his. "No, it doesn't sound dumb. And neither do your plans for raising funds to shelter battered women. I'm very proud of you. I just don't want you to tire yourself."

When Natalie saw Nick had finished his lunch, she scooted around the table and onto his lap. She nuzzled his neck and kissed her way up his chin to his lips. He groaned, and his hand automatically slipped beneath her blouse to caress the slight fullness of her belly. "Your breasts are larger," he muttered in her ear. "I can't wait to taste your milk."

Laughter bubbled up from her throat. "I hope you leave enough for the baby. You have quite an appetite, Nick Jordan."

"I'm a glutton where you're concerned."

Natalie looked anxious for a moment. "I've already started those exercises in the book, Nick, but you realize I'm still going to turn into the world's greatest blimp." Her look was grim. "In fact, they could probably fly me over the next county fair, if they could get me to swallow enough helium."

He smiled at the uncertainty in her eyes. "That's why I insist on your sleeping nude. So I can feel our baby grow." At her look of surprise, he caught her bottom lip between his teeth and nibbled it, then cupped her cheeks between large hands and looked into her eyes. "Natalie, you're going to be the most beautiful woman in the world as far as I'm concerned. I don't care if I have to haul you to the doctor in one of my trucks—"

She slapped him playfully. "I'm not going to get *that* large."

He grinned as his hand slipped farther up her blouse and carefully managed to pull one side of her bra up. He feasted his eyes on the swollen breast. "Sore?" he asked, stroking her gently with one finger.

Natalie lay her head against his shoulder. "Just a tad. But don't stop." Sometimes their lovemaking frightened her. She had never known such happiness. She had never shared such intimacies with a man, nor had she yielded so completely to love.

"Are you sure this is what you want?" Nick whispered, looking into her eyes. "You told me once you intended to remain childless."

"That was in another life," she said, holding his head with one hand, "before I realized love meant taking risks. I'm willing to take them now." They were silent for a moment as Nick continued to worship her other breast.

"My father called this morning," she said, trying to clear her thoughts while Nick tongued the swollen nipple. It was impossible to think straight when he did those things to her. In the beginning she had been afraid of losing control during their lovemaking until she realized that's exactly what

Nick wanted. "He's going to furnish the nursery for us," she said, picking up the thread of her conversation in a throaty voice. She heard Nick groan and laughed. "Of course, it'll probably look like something right out of the Jacobean period and cost a fortune, so I told him I would agree as long as I picked it out. I have to be in Atlanta next month anyway to close on my condo. Nick, are you listening to a word I'm saying?" she asked, feeling a shiver of delight rush up her spine.

"No. Be still so I can kiss the other one again," he said, raising her bra until both creamy breasts fell into his waiting hands. "Lord, you're gorgeous. And you're not going to Atlanta without me. I'm not chancing another freak snowstorm."

"In June?" she asked laughingly. Nevertheless, his protectiveness touched her. She thrust her fingers through his hair and pressed her lips against the thick strands. His hair smelled of soap and sunshine. She gasped aloud as he teased an erect bud with his teeth. "Nick, we shouldn't—"

"We should. And often."

"But what if one of the men needs you?"

"That's why I employ a foreman."

"Well, we're not going to be able to . . . you know, once we hire a housekeeper and someone to help with the baby."

He chuckled. "Why do you think I keep putting it off? Besides, we'll tell her we're newlyweds. She'll *expect* me to be loving you all the time. Making love to you is like tasting a bit of heaven."

"I hope you'll always feel that way."

"Lady, I assure you. It just keeps getting better." Without warning, he stood, capturing her high in his arms.

"What are you doing?"

"I'm going to carry you upstairs and rub your belly until you fall asleep."

"Nick Jordan, you know that never works! I always end up getting . . . you know."

He grinned. "I know."

Nick carried her up the stairs to the bedroom that had at one time belonged to his parents. True to Natalie's promise, she had begun redecorating the house as soon as they'd returned from their honeymoon in Barbados, and the room had been transformed into a suite. The blue and mauve colors were soothing. They had enjoyed frolicking in the large round Jacuzzi, a new addition, where Natalie swore she had conceived.

Nick lay her gently upon the king-size bed that dominated the room. For a long moment he merely stared at her, drinking in the beauty before him. "I hope the baby looks like you," he said, his voice growing husky. "I want him to have your blond hair."

"I was hoping she'd have your hair. It's thicker."

"What are we going to name him?" Nick lay beside her and began stroking her belly.

"I was thinking of Andrea."

"How about Joshua or Samuel? Or Micah?"

"Lord, I never thought I'd see the day Nick Jordan scanned the Bible for baby names." At the dark look he shot her, Natalie snaked her arms around his neck. "We have plenty of time to decide, you know." One hand slowly began unbuttoning hi shirt. His wide chest came into view, and she curled her fingers through the coarse hair. He shrugged off his shirt and tossed it aside. His shoulders were already tan from working in the orchards bare-chested. By the end of the summer, Natalie imagined, they would be baked to a golden brown. She pressed her lips to his breastbone, one of her favorite spots, where she inhaled the scent of soap and maleness. She had learned the tastes and smells of his body, one by one, until they were imbedded in her brain. Even while Nick worked in the orchards, she could call them to mind, and each time her stomach fluttered wildly.

When Natalie finally lay naked before him, Nick gazed at her lovingly. Her stomach was no longer concave—there was a little mound that never ceased to amaze him. He kissed it tenderly. "When will we feel the baby move?"

"In two or three months." It was difficult for Natalie to concentrate with Nick seeking out the pleasure points on her body. He knew her so well. He knew how to bring her to the edge of the universe, and he knew instinctively how to slow her frantic movements and make the moment last. He knew what words whispered in her ear made her hot for him, even though later she would blush at the memory.

At his urging, Natalie began to undress Nick and found him ready and eager for her. But he wouldn't take her now. He would wait. First he used his tongue like an artist, making long deliberate strokes or short fast ones that sent her pulse skyrocketing. He always waited until his wife had unleashed most of her passion before he took her through one final journey.

Nick kissed her long and hard, then moved his lips across each closed eyelid. Natalie often wondered how such a powerful man could be so gentle at times. She had seen his large hands wield heavy machinery, and she had felt them on her skin as light as a butterfly's wing, probing and stroking the very crux of her femininity.

When Nick had her pleading for entry, he moved over her carefully. Their lovemaking was painstakingly slow. No longer did they rush to douse the fire that threatened to consume them as they had in the beginning. Now they used all five senses in their lovemaking. Only when Natalie was satiated did Nick relinquish his control and thrust into the satin folds guardedly. His release was as sweet as her own, Natalie thought, watching the signs of pleasure cross his face. He chanted her name softly. Afterward they held each other until Natalie yawned.

Nick chuckled. "Told you I could make you sleepy, pretty lady."

Natalie smiled and closed her eyes, enjoying the scent that followed their lovemaking. It was sweeter than any perfume, only because of the intense love that had gone into creating it.

Nick would return to the orchards, but not until she slipped off to sleep. In the meantime, he stroked her as she curled against him. "My tigress has finally turned into a kitten," he said, something he teased her about often.

"Don't be so sure of yourself, Nick Jordan. I can still hold my own."

"Face it, lady. I've tamed you just as I said I would."

Natalie opened her eyes and smiled. "I *let* you. But that doesn't mean I'm a pushover, Mister. I can still whip just about any attorney in town, and I have you wrapped around my little finger."

Nick looked amused and raised himself up on one elbow. "Oh, really? When did you discover this?"

Natalie stared at the spot where he'd once had the tattoo bearing Me Lin's name. She had no idea when Nick had had it removed, nor would she have asked him to do so. She knew, though, Me Lin would always be a part of his past, and she didn't resent it. Perhaps his suffering had made him the sensitive, caring man he was once she had managed to crack his protective shell. Each day she noticed that the lines around his eyes and mouth seemed less harsh. He smiled more, laughter seemed to come easily.

"Earth to Natalie. Come in, please."

"Huh?" She blinked.

"I asked you when you first discovered you had me wrapped around your little finger as you claim," he told her.

"When I knew you couldn't live without me, and you couldn't bear the thought of losing me."

He frowned. "I never said all that."

"No, but it was written all over your face. As an attorney, I've learned to read people's faces." Natalie suddenly became pensive.

"What is it?" Nick had learned to read her moods as well.

"What are we going to do when I'm *really* pregnant?"

He looked bemused. "You mean this is a tria run and in reality you've just let your figure go to hell?"

"No, silly. When I get big." She held her hands out as though measuring in her mind how large she was likely to get.

Nick was still baffled. "What do you mean, what are we going to do? I'm probably going to have to wait on you hand and foot so your feet don't swell You'll eat me out of house and home."

She slapped him playfully. "That's not what meant. What are we going to do about you-know what?"

He pondered her words for a moment. "You mean sex?"

"Making love," she corrected him, pursing he lips. "We aren't going to be able to make love nea the end."

Nick gave her a cocky smile and traced her bot tom lip with an index finger. "Lady, I can mak love to you in ways you never dreamed of. And don't even have to unzip my jeans to make you croon."

"Nick Jordan, you're indecent," she said, blush ing.

"I noticed you've picked up a few indecencie yourself, Mrs. Jordan."

"Only at your request," she said smugly. ' wouldn't even consider it with another man."

"I'm glad we agree on one thing."

"Nick, what are you doing?" While they'd been talking, Nick's fingers had busied themselves once more at her breasts.

"All this talk has made me . . . uh . . ."

Her eyes dropped to the growing length between his thighs. "I think I understand."

Nick pulled her up on top of him. "I want to hear you snarl this time, Natalie. I want to feel your fingernails raking across my back. I want you to lose control."

"What about your peaches?"

"To hell with my peaches. I want to see the tigress in you come alive again."

THE EDITOR'S CORNER

There is never a dull moment in our LOVESWEPT offices where we're forever discussing new ideas for the line. So, fair warning, get ready for the fruits of two of our brainstorms . . . which, of course, we hope you will love.

First, expect a fabulous *visual* surprise next month. We are going to reflect the brilliance of our LOVESWEPT author's romances by adding *shimmer* to our covers. Our gorgeous new look features metallic ink frames around our cover illustrations. We've also had a calligrapher devote his talent to reworking the LOVESWEPT lettering into a lacy script and it will be embossed in white on the top metallic border of the books. Each month has a color of its own. (Look for gleaming blue next month . . . for glimmering rosy red the following month.) So what will set apart the books in a given month? Well, the author's name, the book's title, and a tiny decorative border around the art panel will have its own special color. Just beautiful. We've worked long and hard on our new look, and we're popping with prideful enthusiasm for it. Special thanks go to our creative and tireless art director, Marva Martin.

Around here we believe that resting on laurels must be boring (could it also be painful?). And, like most women, all of us LOVESWEPT ladies, authors and editors, are out to prove something as time goes by—namely, *the older we get . . . the better we get . . . in every way!*

Our exciting news has taken so much space that I'm afraid I can give only brief descriptions of the wonderful romances we have coming your way next month. However, I'm sure that just the names of the authors will whet your appetite for the terrific love stories we have in our bright new packages.

Delightful Kay Hooper has come up with a real treat—not just one, but many—the first of which you'll get to sample next month. Kay is writing a number of LOVE-SWEPTs that are based on fairy tales . . . but bringing

(continued)

their themes completely (and excitingly!) up to date. Next month, *Once Upon a Time* . . . **GOLDEN THREADS,** LOVESWEPT #348, tells the love story of Lara Mason who, like Rapunzel, was isolated in a lonely, alien life . . . until Devon Shane came along to help her solve the problems that had driven her into hiding. An absolutely unforgettable romance!

In a book that's as much snappy fun as its title, Doris Parmett gives us **SASSY,** LOVESWEPT #349. Supermodel Sassy Shaw thought she was headed for a peaceful vacation in Nevada, but rancher Luke Cassidy had other plans for his gorgeous guest. This is a real sizzler . . . with lots of guffaws thrown in. We think you'll love it.

The thrilling conclusion of The Cherokee Trilogy arrives from Deborah Smith next month with **KAT'S TALE,** LOVESWEPT #350. Kat Gallatin, whom you've met briefly in the first two of the Cherokee books, is unorthodox . . . to say the least. She's also adorable and heartwarming, a real heroine. That's what Nathan Chatham thinks, too, as he gets involved with the wildcat he wants to see turn kitten in his arms. A fabulous conclusion to this wonderful trio of books—a must read!

Tami Hoag tugs at your heart in **STRAIGHT FROM THE HEART,** LOVESWEPT #351. Jace Cooper, an injured baseball star, was back in town, and Rebecca Bradshaw was desperate to avoid him—an impossibility since she was assigned to be his physical therapist. In this sizzler Rebecca and Jace have to work out the problems of a wild past full of misunderstanding. **STRAIGHT FROM THE HEART** is a sensual and emotional delight from talented Tami.

Patt Bucheister gives us another real charmer in **ELUSIVE GYPSY,** LOVESWEPT #352. Rachel Hyatt is a Justice of the Peace who married Thorn Canon's aunt to some stranger . . . and he's furious when he first encounters her. But not for long. She makes his blood boil (not his temper) and thoroughly enchants him with her

(continued)

off-beat way of looking at the world. Don't miss this marvelous love story!

THE WITCHING TIME, LOVESWEPT #353, by Fayrene Preston is delicious, a true dessert of a romance, so we saved it for the end of LOVESWEPT's September feast. Something strange was going on in Hilary, Virginia. Noah Braxton felt it the second he arrived in town. He knew it when he encountered a golden-haired, blue-eyed witch named Rhiannon York who cast a spell on him. With his quaint aunts, Rhiannon's extraordinary cat, and a mysterious secret in town, Noah finds his romance with the incredible Rhiannon gets unbelievably, but delightfully, complex. A true confection of a romance that you can relish, knowing it doesn't have a single calorie in it to add to your waistline.

We hope you will enjoy our present to you of our new look next month. We want you to be proud of being seen reading a LOVESWEPT in public, and we think you will be with these beautifully packaged romances. Our goal was to give you prettier and more discreet covers with a touch of elegance. Let us know if you think we succeeded.

With every good wish,

Carolyn Nichols

Carolyn Nichols
Editor
LOVESWEPT
Bantam Books
666 Fifth Avenue
New York, NY 10103